Three, Two, One, and . . . ACTION!

I threw my right leg out the window, then my left, and leaped to the ground.

Only my pants didn't.

A belt loop snagged the window latch and caught me suddenly.

"Yeoww!" A superwedgie grabbed me, and I grabbed behind me for the windowsill. This twisting motion didn't relieve the pressure as I thought it would. What it did do was tear a hole in the back of my pants, which dropped me another three inches.

The wedgie dug in deeper. "Yeoww!"

Hearing my cries, the outside cameraman dashed across the lawn, his red camera light flickering.

"No closeups!" I squealed. "Our show is PG!"

Don't Touch that Remote! by Tony Abbott

Episode #1: Sitcom School
Episode #2: The Fake Teacher

Available from MINSTREL Books

Don't Touch that Remote!

EPISODE 2: THE FAKE TEACHER

Tony Abbott

A MINSTREL® BOOK

Published by POCKET BOOKS
New York   London   Toronto   Sydney   Tokyo   Singapore

A MINSTREL PAPERBACK *Original*

A Minstrel Book published by
POCKET BOOKS, a division of Simon & Schuster Inc.
1230 Avenue of the Americas, New York, NY 10020

ISBN: 0-671-02782-4

First Minstrel Books printing November 1999

10 9 8 7 6 5 4 3 2 1

A MINSTREL BOOK and colophon are registered trademarks of
Simon & Schuster Inc.

Front cover photos by Pat Hill Studio

Printed in the U.S.A.

For
the real teachers:
Mr. Strunk, Mr. Pagani, Mrs. Guarnaccia,
Mr. Burr, Mrs. Englander, Mr. Bogg,
Mrs. Duffey, and Mr. Washburn

OPENING TEASER

FADE IN:
OUTSIDE PRESTON WODEHOUSE MIDDLE SCHOOL—MONDAY MORNING

"Could you stand on a box, Spencer?"
"A box?"
"Or a chair."
"You want me to stand on a chair?"
"Maybe a ladder. We need some height."
"I'm afraid of heights."
"Just two steps. The top. Sit at the top."
"You want me to sit at the top of a ladder?"
"And then jump."

It was first thing Monday morning.
I was standing on the front wheelchair ramp of

my school, having this weird conversation with a cigar-toting man named Leonard Shell.

He's the producer of the TV show I'm the star of—*The Spencer Babbitt Show.* It's on Saturday nights at eight.

The show is named after me, but I'm not the boss.

"You want me to jump off the ladder?"

"Gives you more control than falling," he said.

I nearly choked. "Falling! It's a sitcom. What's wrong with just saying funny lines?"

Mr. Shell waved his cigar at the camera operators and lighting people and makeup staff rushing around like crazy. "Spencer, our show needs more *vrrmm!*"

I stared at the man. "Vrrmm. Is that a technical TV term, or were you just clearing your throat?"

He chuckled and shook his head. "Here's the problem. That new action show, *ER Cops,* is on the same time as us. Lots of running, dashing, jumping. To keep our audience, we need action, too. You know, vrrmm! Like something fast. You gotta have action, Spencer. You don't want people reaching for their remotes."

Ah. Remotes.

This was like the main evil thing in televisionland.

That people watching your show will get bored, reach for the remote, and—*flick!*—you're history.

"So, how about this," Mr. Shell went on. "You jump from the ladder, only it seems like you fall, and then—vrrmm!—your friends dash to the rescue . . ."

Ah. My friends.

If you didn't tune in to our first episode, let me bring you up to speed. After Mr. Shell bought my school—that's right, *bought* my school—to tape the show in, he made me and my friends the stars.

Cameras follow Pam Scott, Danny Domper, Jay Freeman, and me all around the school, our homes, and on location, taping the stuff that happens to us. At the end of the week, we have our show.

If you saw the first episode, you'll know that my friends are severely nutty, while I am perfectly normal.

". . . then you collapse!" Mr. Shell said, swinging his arms all around. "Everyone laughs and laughs, and we roll the credits! Is that good or what?"

I was about to say *or what,* when someone tramped up behind us.

"Ah . . . ah . . . Spencer?"

Enter Principal Pangborn, huffing his usual huff. He's another member of the cast, but he's our real principal. Actually, he's our really great principal. The best.

But ever since our show's been on, he's been losing sleep and hair worrying about the school's reputation.

He looked sleepy now. His hair was thinner, too.

That can mean only one thing. Upper Case time.

"Spencer," he said, "I think this week's episode should focus on Teaching. For instance, the Big Essay Contest this week—"

"Teaching is for PBS. Our Show needs Vrrmm!" Mr. Shell said, using upper case, initials, *and* sound effects.

I phased out. You see, there is this little war going on between my producer and my principal about who's really the boss of me. I'm a TV star, but I'm also a student. I have Responsibilities. Not to mention Parents, a Dog, and, of course, Best Friends.

"Move your big feet, Clowny. I'm gonna tell him!"

"I spotted them first, Stubbylegs!"

[CUT TO: TWO KIDS, one tall and thin, one short and chubbyish, NUDGING each other up the sidewalk]

My friends, Jay and Danny, right on cue.

"Did you see?" Danny blurted out, jabbing his

thumb over his shoulder. "Dee Weiden and her galpals."

I glanced over the bank of cameras and lights at a huddle of sixth- and seventh-grade girls.

"Fans, Spencer," Jay said. *"Girl* fans."

"And Dee's mine," said Danny.

"Really? In what dimension?" Jay said casually.

Danny ignored that. "I'm going to wave. TV is cool. Dee will see me and think I'm cool, too. I'll wave."

Jay gargled a sort of laugh in his throat. "If you were Mr. Freeze, she wouldn't think you were cool, Gumby. You are totally *under* her radar!"

"Don't start with me, Skeletor!" Danny snorted.

"CUT!" I held up my hands. "What is this, the Legion of Numbskulls? We're taping a scene here. Where is Pam, anyway? She's supposed to enter soon."

"Working with Mrs. Brady on the contest," Jay said.

"The essay contest, exactly!" Principal Pangborn suddenly erupted. "I'm also starting a program of visits to a nursing home. I call it SHARE—Students Helping the Aged with Respect and Empowerment. Dr. Florence Goodwin, who runs the home, is Mrs. Brady's sister. We think Project SHARE is a perfect idea for your show."

Another thing I get is everybody's perfect ideas for the show. It's the price you pay for being on TV.

"Nursing homes is good," Mr. Shell said, "but first, Spencer does a little sharing with the ladder."

"Uh . . . uh . . ." I stammered. But before I could run, dash, or jump out of the way, the ladder was there.

[CUT TO: TWO MEN, running up the sidewalk]

Totally on cue, Dickens and Fenster, the two workmen from our first episode, ran up with a short ladder.

The makeup lady dusted my face. The camera people zoomed in to start the scene. And Mr. Shell grinned.

"Three, two, one, and—vrrmm!" he shouted.

Vrrmm? He meant Action. And he got it.

As soon as I reached the top of the ladder—*bang!*

[CUT TO: school doors blasting open]

Totally *not* on cue, Pam Scott bolted down the stairs, screaming at the top of her lungs.

PAM

Mrs. Brady's going to have a baby!
NOW! IN THE CLASSROOM!

Weee-ooo-weee-ooo! Already an ambulance was roaring into the parking lot. Three paramedics jumped out with one of those stretchers on wheels. They rolled it right up the front ramp and into our opening scene.

ME

Whoa! I should probably get off—

"HI!" Danny cried suddenly, finally getting the nerve to wave at Dee Weiden. Except it wasn't a wave. It was more of a punch at the air. And it wasn't air he punched. It was my ladder. *Thwonk!* His stubby arm thrust into the rungs like a piston.

"Help!" I yelled.

My three friends whirled around and held the ladder steady. While I fell off.

Wump! I slammed onto the speeding stretcher, rolled off the other side, and smacked the ground like a sack of stones. "Yeooow!" I shrieked.

Dee and her friends burst into giggles as my friends set the ladder gently on the grass.

Peering down, Jay said, "You should have jumped."

"You get much more control, Spencer," Pam added.

I scowled up at them. "Thanks for breaking the

ladder's fall, so that *my* fall wouldn't break the ladder!"

"That's a funny line," Danny said.

The medics rushed Mrs. Brady out of school and into the ambulance. They tore from the parking lot. *Vrrmm!*

Mr. Shell jumped with glee. "Is this good or what?"

FADE OUT:

END OF TEASER

ACT ONE

FADE IN:
SCENE 1: SCHOOL HALL—OUTSIDE MEDIA CENTER

"Why are you walking so funny?" Jay asked me.

I turned to him. "Oh, I don't know. Maybe because . . . um . . . I fell off a ladder!"

Jay, Danny, and I were headed for the media center, which in our school is also the library. It was the beginning of second period, an hour after the ladder incident.

"Sorry about that," Danny said. "But Mr. Shell is right about one thing. *ER Cops* is one incredible actionfest."

"Isn't that on the same time as our show?" Jay asked.

"Yes, it is," I said. "Did you tape it?"

Danny shook his head. "No tape. I tell you, that show is so cool; a total, wall-to-wall, nonstop—"

"Wait a second," I said, holding up my hand. "If *ER Cops* is on the same time as our show and you didn't tape it, then how do you know what it's like? Unless . . . whoa! *You didn't watch our show!* That's it! You're a traitor to all we believe in! You're a . . . a . . . fake friend!"

"No, I'm not," Danny protested. "I watched both shows at the same time."

A moment of silence while we processed that.

"Two TVs?" Jay said finally. "That's futuristic."

Danny shook his head again. "No, one TV."

I looked him squarely in the eye. "Then how?"

He smiled. "Take a look at this."

[CUT TO: closeup of Danny's right hand]

His thumb was red in one spot, like a small bruise.

"The remote," Danny said, grinning. "I flick between two channels. I go back and forth so fast— I get both shows! I don't miss a scene, I don't miss a single line. When I'm really cooking, it's truly amazing. For a second on Saturday night I changed channels so fast, it actually seemed as if Spencer went from our show—zoom!—right onto one of those ER stretchers!"

"That actually happened, Danny," I said flatly.

"Oh. I knew I saw it somewhere."

I grumbled as we continued down the hall. "Well, just don't tell Mr. Shell about your dorky new talent. He's scared enough as it is. If he thinks everybody can do what you do, he'll have me jumping from airplanes by the final scene."

"That'd give the people some vrrmm!" Jay added.

When we stepped into the media center, I stopped short. "Shhh—"

Zrrrr! Hooo! Snap! A strange sequence of sounds met us at the door. A sudden, high-pitched whine, followed by a loud breath, followed by a sharp cracking sound.

Zrrrr! Hooo! Snap!

"What is that?" I whispered.

"Darth Vader using an electric drill while eating Doritos in our library?" Danny said, chuckling at Jay.

I put my finger to my lips and motioned to a figure seated at a desk behind the rows of book stacks. Slowly, we edged along the shelves.

Zrrrr! Hooo! Snap! It was Pam, sitting alone at a desk.

She looked up slowly. Her long brown hair was

chopped and messy as usual. She was her normal, I guess, non-ugly self, in T-shirt and khaki shorts.

But her eyes! They burned like fire.

"Pam, are you okay?"

Without shifting her fiery gaze from me, she reached into a cardboard box and removed a brand-new pencil.

Then she jammed the pencil into an electric sharpener—*zrrrr!*—until it was sharper than a needle, blew the pencil dust off the new tip—*hooo!*—then slowly and deliberately—*snap!*—broke the pencil in half.

"So I guess you're not okay," I said, gulping. "But why are you doing that to those poor pencils?"

Pam sucked in a long breath. "I don't need them anymore, do I? Mrs. Brady was supposed to help me with my essay. . . ."

"She had a baby," Jay said.

"SHE HAD SIX BABIES!" Pam screamed. "SHE HAD A WHOLE *BUNCH* OF BABIES!"

Zrrrrrrrrrrrr! Pam thrust another pencil into the sharpener and kept it there until only the eraser was left.

"The big essay contest is Thursday night," she went on. "I'm supposed to read in front of the whole school. But I don't have an essay. I don't have a topic. I don't have anything! And now she's in the hospital!''

"Hey," I said, "did you know that Mrs. Brady's sister runs the Coconut Palms Rest Villa that's doing the Project SHARE thing with Principal Pangborn?"

Pam glared at me. "So what?"

I shrugged. "I just think it's funny, that's all."

"Funny?" she repeated. "You want funny?"

Zrrrr! Hooo! Snap!

It was the way Pam made the pencils perfect before breaking them in half that struck me as really scary.

"We're signed up for the nursing home tonight," Danny said. "Why don't you come and write about that?"

"I can't," Pam growled. "I'm in the American History category. I picked history because it's the principal's favorite subject and I thought I'd score some points."

"You've already got honors," said Jay. "How many points do you need?"

"All of them!" Pam said sharply. She cocked her arm back, aiming another blunt pencil at the sharpener.

It was clear she needed something. Brilliance struck.

"Pam, wait," I said. "I . . . I . . . I have an

idea. You can help pick a new teacher. You can personally choose someone who could still help you with your essay."

Pam set the pencil down unsharpened. "Really?"

I nodded. "Principal Pangborn told me that he and Miss Krabbiker are interviewing substitutes tomorrow morning first thing. They're letting me watch because of the show."

Pam's shoulders relaxed. "And maybe I could come?"

"Absolutely," I said, trying to lift her out of the black hole she was in. "Think about it, Pam. Think about choosing a great teacher. Think about getting help on your essay. Think about standing in the courtyard, reading your prize-winning essay to rounds and rounds of applause. Think about people tossing flowers!"

Pam brightened. "Flowers? You promise?"

I gulped. "Well, just think about it for now. I'll meet you after first period tomorrow. Teachers' Lounge."

"It's a deal," Pam said.

But as we broke out our books and began studying, Pam stuffed her box of new pencils into her backpack.

"Just in case," she said quietly.

SCENE 2: COCONUT PALMS REST VILLA— MONDAY AFTER SUPPER

The rest of the day went pretty much without a hitch, except that Principal Pangborn told me at least four times that he hoped the SHARE program at Coconut Palms would be great for my show. "Because sharing with seniors is great for our school!"

Right. No pressure or anything.

Then Leonard Shell called me twice at home to say he was sending cameramen to the nursing home, but was still thinking of ways to spice up the action on the show.

"Vrrmm, Spencer, vrrmm!" was the way he put it.

Sometimes it seemed like I was caught between two barking dogs. Shell and Pangborn. Bulldog and pitbull.

Ah, the life of a star.

Mr. Shell was right about keeping people from using remotes, though. I found this out when Danny and his father picked up Jay and me for our nursing-home visit.

"Loved your first show, Spencer," Mr. Domper said as we hopped into the backseat next to Danny.

"Thanks," I said. "I know Danny watched *ER*

Cops at the same time, so I'm glad you actually understood what was going on."

"I did and it was great! Especially when Miss Krabbiker did that lung transplant on the other teacher and The Tank squashed you into the emergency room just before the gym wall fell down and all those cops saw the principal kissing that nurse? That was terrific!"

I gave Danny a harsh look. "Things seem to have gotten a little mixed up, huh? Nice work, Thumbsy."

He grinned. "I prefer to be called . . . Danny The Flick." He held up his stupid thumb. The weird red callous had grown larger since that morning.

A few minutes later we rolled into the parking lot of the Coconut Palms Rest Villa.

Jay whistled when we passed the sign. "What a cool name for a rest home. It makes you want to live here."

I chuckled. "Just remember, SHARE is Pangborn's baby. Dr. Goodwin who runs this place has won tons of awards and stuff. Translation: if we mess up, I'll hear about it until I'm old enough to go here."

"Hey, we know how to act," Danny said.

"Act up, maybe," I said. "Just try to be polite."

Coconut Palms was one of those older mansions you see around Hollywood. I'd read that it had once been a silent movie star's house. Now it had a couple of modern wings attached, but old places like that always needed work. Hanging over the entrance was a low roof made of red tiles, a few of which looked broken and cracked.

"I wonder if those tiles ever fall on people," Jay said.

"Ouch!" said Danny. "Good for business, though. The roof falls, and you're an instant patient."

For some reason, that made me think of Mr. Shell.

After we climbed out of the car, one of the scene's cameramen waved from the sidewalk. He lifted the camera to his shoulder and followed us to the front doors.

There I spotted an elderly woman dressed in green, struggling to get the heavy doors open from the inside.

"Politeness, remember?" I said.

I pulled the door open and held it for the nice lady.

"Thank you, dear," she replied.

"You're welcome," I said, glancing back at Jay and Danny so that they would get the idea about how to act. "Were you visiting someone, ma'am?"

17

"No, but I will now," she said with a laugh. Then she scampered quickly over a hedge. "Toodaloo!"

"I hope I can jump like that at her age," Jay said.

"You see?" I said, winking at the camera. "Politeness works wonders. The principal will be proud of that."

Danny laughed to himself. "We are doing great!"

A moment later, two Hefty bag–size guys in blue jackets bolted out the door, nearly knocking us down.

"Out of my way!" one snapped.

"Me left, you right!" the other grunted. They tramped away across the grass and were gone.

"Now that was *not* polite," Jay said directly into the camera. "Notice the difference."

As soon as we entered the building a woman in a white uniform stormed up the hall at us. "I am Nurse Sternwood," she said sternly.

"Oh, hi," I said. "We're here for the—"

"Did you help a patient escape the building just now?" she interrupted. "Hmm? Did you?"

I looked wide-eyed back at Jay and Danny. They looked at me the same way. The cameraman shrugged.

"Es-es-escape?" I said. "A patient escaped? Um . . . could you describe her?"

"Her?" the nurse said. "I never said it was a woman."

Something went *pop!* in my ears. Right away I knew we had done something wrong. I could see it now. I could hear it already, even before I got back to school.

PRINCIPAL PANGBORN
Spencer! This is horrible! Horrible!

My brain scanned at light speed for the right thing to say to the nurse, but it just wasn't quick enough.

"It could have been a man," Jay said. "Definitely."

No . . . no . . . no . . . my brain cried out silently.

"Then you *did* see someone," the nurse stated.

Pop-pop-pop! went my ears.

Danny, who had been quiet up till now, stepped forward. "You mean today?" he blurted out.

"What . . . ?" the nurse said, as mystified as I was.

Danny pressed on. "Because I have to say, if you mean today, I'm pretty sure we didn't see anybody."

My lips opened to make a sound. "Shhh . . . shhh."

"Especially no lady in a green bathrobe," Danny said.

"Who said she was wearing a green bathrobe!"

"SHH—SHARE!" I yelped suddenly. "SHARE! SHARE! We're here for THE SHARE PROGRAM!"

That silenced things for a few seconds.

Then a sort of grinding sound, as the nurse struggled to shift mental gears. "SHARE? From the middle school? Oh. SHARE. Yes. Dr. Goodwin's project with the school. Fine. Well. Follow me."

I swatted Danny's arm quietly as we followed the nurse up the main stairs. "Numbskull!" I hissed.

Two floors up we came out into a wide hall with numbered rooms. Lots of older people in green bathrobes, some with canes and wheelchairs, waved at us.

"We're supposed to meet Dr. Goodwin," I said.

The nurse made a noise. "Dr. Goodwin is off for a few days to help her sister and her family."

"Of course!" Jay said. "Six babies. Makes sense—"

"And I'm in control until she returns!"

Control. For some reason, I knew it was one of Nurse Sternwood's upper-case words.

"Lots of people say *I'm* a control freak," I said.

Nurse Sternwood stopped and turned slowly to me. *"Freak?* Is that supposed to be what you students consider—*funny?"*

I looked into her dark staring eyes. "Um,

actually . . . no. Not funny. Very unfunny, in fact. I'll shut up now.''

The nurse then told me that the person I was assigned—''an older woman last seen wearing a green bathrobe''—was temporarily missing.

''Imagine that,'' I mumbled.

''Until she is found—and she *will* be found—you will have to double up with one of your friends.''

She consulted her clipboard. ''Danny Domper, you have room three-thirteen, Mrs. Burke. Jay Freeman, room three-fifteen, Mr. Wiggins. I grounded three-fifteen this morning for eating between meals. I run a tight ship, now that Dr. Goodwin is away. Obey my rules and things will be fine!''

She marched away, leaving us staring at a white sheet of paper taped to the wall. It was entitled New Rules.

> *1. No food after 6 p.m.*
> *2. No noise after 7 p.m.*
> *3. No lights after 8 p.m.*

''Brutal,'' Jay muttered. ''I mean, Disneyland, it's not.''

''I thought this place was so cool,'' Danny said.

I gulped. ''I think it was until Nurse Sternwood took over. I guess that's what she means when she says she runs a tight ship. I wonder if she's got a dungeon."

Danny looked at me and Jay. "So, now what? It's six-thirty. What should I do with my person for a half hour?"

"Stuff," Jay said. "Things you do with your grandparents. Play cards, play bingo, do a craft, sing songs."

Danny coughed a laugh. "This is a rest home. You don't want to hear me sing."

He peeked into Mrs. Burke's room. "Uh . . . hello? I'm Danny Domper? From the middle school—"

A small elderly woman rolled her wheelchair to the door. She had white hair done up in a Dairy Queen swirl. Her face was chubby and bright. "I'm Helen Burke," she said. "Oh, look at your cheeks, Danny! Plump as peaches!"

"And he loves to have them pinched." Jay snickered.

"No, wait!" said Danny, backing away. "No . . . no!"

But the woman lunged like a panther at Danny's cheeks, grasping them tightly between her fingers. "Oooh! Say, Danny, a bunch of us are going down to the TV room to fight over programs. Want to join us?"

Danny's eyes twinkled suddenly. He cocked an eyebrow. "Did you say . . . fight over programs? Oh, Mrs. Burke, I think I've got exactly what you need." He held up that bulging thumb of his. It looked like some kind of deli product.

She chuckled. "Then let's hurry—before they shut down the wide screen!"

As Danny wheeled her to the elevator, Mrs. Burke turned to Jay and me. "Good luck with Scroogie!"

I glanced at Jay. "Scroogie? You think she means your guy?"

Jay made a face and knocked lightly on the next door. "Uh . . . Mr. Wiggins?"

A voice snarled from inside the room.

"Oh, thanks a lot for coming—while I'm still alive!"

SCENE 3: COCONUT PALMS—ROOM 315—
MONDAY P.M.

The guy was one of the smallest, palest, thinnest
men I'd ever seen. He was sitting on his bed with
his skinny legs dangling off the side.

"What are you staring at, Pretty Boy?" he barked.
I stepped back. "I . . . uh . . ."

"And you with the bird hair, what's your name?"
"Jay."

"J? What is this, *Wheel of Fortune?* You going to
give it to me a letter at a time? Do I have to buy
a vowel? Here's a lung."

"No, his name is Jay," I said. "J-A-Y."

"Why? I'll tell you why," the man grumbled.
"I'm so old, every morning I read the obituaries. If
my name's not there, I get dressed. I'm so old,
when I bend down to tie my shoelaces, I try and
think of other stuff to do while I'm down there."

Jay chuckled. "You have a nice room, though."

"Nice room? The walls are so thin I can read
over Burkie's shoulder! And, boy, has she got lousy
taste in books! Speaking of taste, the dining room
used to be air-conditioned. But since Sternwood
shut it off, I've never seen air in that condition. You
barely see your food. And not seeing your food is
a good thing. Since Dr. Goodwin left, it looks terri-

ble and tastes bad. The worst part is, they hardly give you any! Boy, I'd love some nachos!"

Mr. Wiggins stopped for a moment to breathe.

I didn't know whether to run or sit back and enjoy the show. The guy was talking so fast, my brain was getting tired just keeping up. But he was funny.

"Were you ever in show business?" I asked.

"Ever hear of the Marx Brothers?" he said, bouncing from his bed to look out the window.

"You're one of the Marx Brothers?" Jay gasped.

"No, I'm one of the Wiggins brothers. But I taught the Marx Brothers' kids. I was a teacher. Then I took a shine to the shoe business. I got booted out of that. Then I was in the sock business. That was full of holes. Now I just wear slippers and eat peaches."

Jay cracked up. "So, Mr. Wiggins, I guess you really don't like it here."

"Call me Wiggy," the man answered. "Truth is, I complain, but Coconut Palms is a great place to be. At least when Dr. Goodwin is around. But since Sternwood took over, our rest home is more like a rest-in-peace home!"

I nodded. "She does seem a little harsh."

"Harsh?" he said. "When Sternwood was a kid,

her *parents* ran away from home! But I'm onto her. That's why she doesn't like me."

"We'll have to think of a way to help," said Jay.

Jay, thinking? "But, Jay, remember Pangborn—"

Wham! Something hit the door. It was Danny.

"I forgot the rules!" he cried. "Two big guys chased us out of the cafeteria!"

"I thought you were in the TV room," I said.

"We got hungry!" Danny replied, his eyes showing fear. "You know how TV makes you hungry. Especially if you're exercising."

"You were exercising?" Wiggy asked.

"Our thumbs!" Danny cried. "Everyone loved the flick! Now the guards are after us. Can I hide here?"

Wiggy motioned to the floor. "Under the bed. By the way, I dropped half a Spam sandwich there this morning, when they caught me eating real food."

"Spam is real food?" Danny asked.

"More real than the goop Sternwood serves!" Wiggy said. "Find it and I'll split it with you."

NURSE STERNWOOD'S VOICE
(FROM HALL) **Where are those kids? One of them raided the cafeteria. And I'm sure that chatty one helped our patient escape!**

"Yikes!" I gasped. I jumped for the closet but Jay squeezed in first. I panicked. "Danny, you got room?"

"It's a bed, not a condo! Find your own hiding place."

I pushed my way under the bed anyway. Wiggy's Spam sandwich was there, too. And judging by the way it smelled, it was as old as he was.

Nurse Sternwood clomped in. "Where did they go?"

"Your good looks?" Wiggins said. "I never knew you had any!"

The nurse grumbled. "I'll find those kids, especially that TV troublemaker. He seems like the ringleader. The others look too stupid to pick their noses."

I grinned at Danny. For revenge, he flicked the sandwich closer to my nose.

The nurse turned on her heels and left the room.

"Is it safe to come out?" I whispered.

"I'll let you know when the coast is clear," Wiggy said. Jay edged out of the closet and mumbled something I couldn't hear. Then both of them snuck out into the hall.

That left Danny and me jammed under the bed, breathing the thick smell of very old, very ripe Spam.

SCENE 4: WIGGY'S ROOM—MINUTES LATER

"One more whiff of Mr. Spammo," I grunted, "and I'm gonna hurl!"

It was ten minutes later. Danny's face was red.

"It's mutating, Spencer. I think it moved."

"That would explain the b.o.," I said. "I'm out!"

Danny and I scrambled from under the stinky bed, snorting to try and clear our noses.

"Some pal Jay turned out to be," I said.

We tiptoed to the door and peeked out.

"We'll have a better chance if we split up," Danny said. "Try to make it to my dad's car before Nurse Sternwood and her death squad see us. Good luck."

Danny slunk out of the room when the hall was empty. I wasn't so lucky. The two massive hulks we saw at the entrance appeared at one end of the hall.

I got inspired. I grabbed Wiggy's bathrobe, hung it on my shoulders, and shuffled back into the hall and away from the two men. I was hunched over, like a TV actor pretending to be an old man. I hoped it would work.

At the corner I saw a door. I pushed it open. It was dark, but I could see steps leading down at the far end. I slipped through the door and started for the stairs.

"Hey."

I stopped. There was a man standing in the shadows halfway down the short hall. His face was hidden. I darted back and hunched over, hiding my own face.

"Are you escaping?" he whispered. "Patients try to escape all the time now. They don't like the new rules."

I needed to get to the stairs, but he wasn't moving. I disguised my voice. "Is there a way out . . . sonny?"

"Lots," the guy whispered again. "But you're not allowed in this part of the Villa. They'll catch you."

And then what? I thought. *The dungeon?* But I was casual. "You're going to get caught, too."

"Who, me?" he said. "I don't think so."

"Why not?"

"I'm Nurse Sternwood's head of security. That's how I know you're not supposed to be here."

I gulped and started to sweat my usual large dollops.

Head of security? This shadow guy was the enemy.

"And guess what?" he went on. "I'm looking for a patient in a green bathrobe."

I looked down. Yeah, that stupid green bathrobe thing again. But what to do? If I proved I wasn't a patient, he'd know I was the kid who helped the lady escape. And I couldn't just outrun him. I needed a diversion.

That was when my fingers got slimy.

In the left pocket of Wiggy's bathrobe was the other half of that half-rotten Spam sandwich. In fact, judging by the slime and the emerging stink, this half-rotten half was more half-rotten than the other half-rotten half.

Maybe it was the even more half-rotten half of an even older rotten whole that I hadn't found yet.

Anyway, as half of my brain was working on this problem, the other half was doing a not-half-bad job of trying to get me out of my situation. It had an idea.

"What's that?" I suddenly thought to say.

"What's what?" the head of security said.

I tossed the hunk of mutant Spam into the shadows at him, turned, and ran.

"Agkkk!" the security guy cried. "HEY! STOP!"

I shot back through the door and down the corridor to where I thought the main stairs were.

"There he is! Get him!" the two hulking orderlies yelled. They charged toward me. I spun and ran.

All of a sudden Mrs. Burke was there, edging out of her room in her wheelchair. "Making a break for it?"

"I'm trying!"

"Take the main stairs!" she said, then she jerked her wheelchair in front of the two muscle dudes.

"Ooof!" One nearly got spiked on the handles, while the other squeaked by, sending her chair into a spin.

"Just wait till bingo night!" she shrieked, as they charged for me once again.

"I'll stop them for ya!" yelled another patient, entering the hall from his room. He reached into his mouth, pulled out a double set of gleaming white chompers, and lobbed them at the orderlies.

[CUT TO: closeup of jumbo chattering teeth approaching at high velocity]

Clack! Clack! Clack! went the teeth.

"Yikes!" The two guys ducked at the last minute and the teeth sailed into a group of doctors tramping up the stairs.

"Incoming!" one of them hollered, and they went down like bowling pins. The teeth clamped onto one doctor's leg. He clutched it, howling, "Doctor! Doctor!"

I dashed quickly for the main stairs.

Suddenly, leaping at me from ten yards away was the security guy, screaming into a walkie-talkie. "Shut the exits!"

[CUT TO: side hallway]

At this point, Nurse Sternwood charged toward me out of nowhere, yelling, "I'll get you!"

Uh-oh. A bad guy sandwich! Worse than Spam!

I could either rely on special effects to make me vanish—which wasn't likely, since all that stuff is computerized and doesn't happen in real life anyway—or find an actual exit. When I leaped down the stairs, I noticed that the window halfway down the steps was open.

Without another thought, I jumped up to the sill. Peering down, I saw it was only eight feet to the ground.

"Vrrrmm!" I cried. I tossed the bathrobe away, threw my right leg out the window, then my left, and leaped to the ground.

Only my pants didn't.

A belt loop snagged the window latch and caught me suddenly.

"Yeoww!" A superwedgie grabbed me, and I

grabbed behind me for the windowsill. This twisting motion didn't relieve the pressure as I thought it would. What it did do was tear a hole in the back of my pants, which dropped me another three inches.

The wedgie dug in deeper. "Yeoww!"

Hearing my cries, the outside cameraman dashed across the lawn, his red camera light flickering.

"No closeups!" I squealed. "Our show is PG!"

At that moment, two things happened. First, four more security guards rushed into the stairwell from every direction, and, second, I spotted someone wheeling a large laundry cart down the sidewalk below.

It's amazing how a crisis will shift what's important for you. I never would have guessed that at some point in my life I would be hoping my pants would rip entirely off me so that I could plummet top speed into a pile of dirty towels.

But now?

It was be captured or be pantless.

I said a bad word and let go of the sill.

[SOUND EFFECTS: sound of ripping cloth: KRRIPPPP!]

Like a crash-test dummy, I launched away from the window and crumpled into the laundry cart with a soft squishing sound.

I looked up to see who my savior was.

"Jay?"

He grinned. "Just sharing, like I'm supposed to."

As the cameraman lunged closer, I pulled a dirty towel over me—like criminals pull jackets over their heads when newspeople zoom in.

The towel smelled pretty bad.

"Spam!" I coughed.

SCENE 5: TEACHERS' LOUNGE—TUESDAY A.M.

"Are you limping, Spencer?"

"No." In fact, I *was* limping, but wearing pants at least, when I met Pam outside the Teachers' Lounge the next morning. Even though my smelly-towel landing had been soft, the wedgie experience so soon after the ladder experience left me hobbling a bit.

"So, how did it go at the nursing home last night?"

"It went," I said.

"I heard you were . . . under."

"Under?" I said, puzzled. "Under where?"

"Exactly!" Pam laughed.

I gave her the evil eye. "An underwear joke! So the guys blabbed the whole thing, huh? And how's your history essay coming?"

Pam's laugh died. "Uck. My grades will be history if I don't have it written by Thursday."

"Exactly," I said with a laugh. "So let's hire a teacher."

We entered the Lounge.

Principal Pangborn rose from a long brown table. "Ah, Spencer, Pam. Glad you could join us. Unofficially of course." He indicated two chairs for us.

The camerawoman was in position in the back.

Sitting next to the principal was Miss Krabbiker, wearing her usual long black dress. Her white hair was piled on top of her head in a sort of cone. "We have three applicants for the position of long-term substitute for Mrs. Brady's social studies class," she said.

The principal then turned to me. "By the way, Spencer, do you know who lost his pants at the Coconut Palms Rest Villa last night? Nurse Sternwood seemed to think it was a SHARE student."

My blood went icy cold. I was torn between telling my principal the horrible story in every grisly detail, and trying to forget the whole messy thing ever happened. What I came out with was, "Uh . . . uh . . ."

"Spencer was sharing so much of himself," Pam said, with a wink at me, "he probably didn't even notice."

"Ah!" The principal smiled broadly. "That's the whole purpose of SHARE, isn't it?" He rubbed his hands together eagerly. "And now your TV audience will get to see Education at work, too. Choosing the best Teacher!"

At that, Pam sort of rippled with glee. She gave us all a big smile. "This is going to be great! I can't wait!"

"I agree!" the principal oozed. "Great, great, great!"

Now, I don't know about you, but when I see people on TV acting very excited and hopeful about something they want to happen—I know it's not going to happen.

Some sort of plot twist is just waiting to twist.

Otherwise, it would be Boring.

And Boring has folks flicking their Remotes.

But everyone was looking at me to chime in with a chirpy, upbeat line. So, in the immortal words of Leonard Shell, I said, "Three, two, one, and . . . *vrrmm!*"

Tap, tap, tap. A soft knocking came on the door.

We all turned to see candidate number one.

"Whoa!" I murmured under my breath.

[CUT TO: closeup of a YOUNG MAN in the doorway]

First of all, the guy must have borrowed his blazer from the Incredible Hulk. It was way too big for him. Under it he was wearing a T-shirt that might have had some color—maybe—ten years ago. Faded isn't quite the word. Below the T-shirt were bright green swim trunks. His hair was long, blond, and tied in a ponytail.

Judging by the peach fuzz on his cheeks, he couldn't have been more than three or four years older than me.

Typical teacher type? I don't think so.

He put out his hand for someone to shake.

"My name is, like, you know . . . Bob?"

Principal Pangborn shook the limp thing. "I . . . er . . . suppose it is. Please take a seat."

"Take it where?" Bob said. Then he got it. "Oh . . . you mean sit. Cool."

Pam's big smile started to wobble, then died completely because of what Bob did next. The head tilt.

What I mean is that the instant Bob sat down at the end of the table, he tilted his head sharply to one side.

And raised his hand. But not into the air. To his face.

[CUT TO: Bob's hand]

We watched him jam his right index finger deep into his left nostril.

Pam jolted as if her seat were wired to a power line.

"Ah . . . well . . ." Principal Pangborn shuffled papers nervously. Then he asked his first question.

PRINCIPAL PANGBORN

How long have you been teaching, Bob?

BOB

Counting today? Like . . . a day.

The principal blinked, then glanced over at Miss K.

MISS KRABBIKER

Yes . . . well, I see you've never taken any teaching courses. What exactly brings you to education?

BOB

My mom. She dropped me off.

I laughed under my breath. Pam let out a low puff of air. The camerawoman adjusted the focus and zoomed in on Bob's right hand as he slowly reached up again and dug his middle finger into the same nostril.

BOB

I really really like to surf. But to, like, do that all the time you need scads of dough and stuff. So I'm gonna work a really really lot before I get, like, there.

PRINCIPAL PANGBORN

(PUZZLED) I'm sorry . . . get where?

BOB

Like, you know . . . there?

Bob dislodged his finger and held it up to look at.

Principal Pangborn's super-bushy eyebrows met over his nose and his eyes shrank as if he were witnessing the end of civilization right here in the Teachers' Lounge.

So when Bob lifted his thumb up and began tilting his head to allow access to his other nostril, Principal Pangborn bolted up from his chair. "Yes, well . . . thank you."

"Cool," Bob said, holding out his hand to shake. "So, like, when do I start?"

The principal's face creased in horror as he shrank away from the hand. "We'll . . . get back to you."

"Dude!"

After Bob slouched from the room, Miss K fixed her eyes at the clock on the wall, grasped her wrist, and began taking her own pulse.

Principal Pangborn wiped his forehead. "I don't think he has the level of experience we're looking for."

"So, I guess Bob snot the one," I said, to be funny.

Pam's eyeballs went fiery at me again. "Candidate number two had better be better, Spencer."

That's when music started to pound in the hall. It was coming from the auditorium.

SCENE 6: AUDITORIUM—MOMENTS LATER

Thumpa-thumpa-jang-jang!

When we stepped into the auditorium, the lights dimmed. The curtains ruffled aside, the spotlight came on, and out came a woman.

Imagine a lipstick supermodel slinking across the stage in our auditorium. Imagine her, because I did.

"Joy," the young woman said. "I'm Joy."

My grin shot around behind my ears. "You sure are."

"Joy . . . Starr." The "ah" sound when she said her last name seemed to go on for about a minute and a half. I was loving it, until I felt a major stinging sensation on my arm. Pam was slapping it repeatedly.

"Pull your tongue back in, you doofus," she said. "She's as bad as Booger Bob!"

We all slunk into the first row.

Pam began drumming her fingers on the seat arm.

MISS KRABBIKER
Miss Starr, this position is for a long-term substitute in social studies.

JOY STARR
I'm *verrrry* social! And I can study, watch!

She then wrinkled her forehead and put her hand on her chin as if she were reading a Dr Pepper label for calories. She broke from that pose with a big smile.

JOY STARR

See?

Principal Pangborn shuffled some papers again. Pam began tapping her foot.

PRINCIPAL PANGBORN

Can you teach seventh-grade geography?

"Of course!" Joy stuck out her fingers and drew a big rectangle in the air. "Here's Colorado. I can also do Wyoming, watch." She drew another big air rectangle.

Pam's fidgeting went into overdrive, both hands and feet drumming and tapping like a marching band.

MISS KRABBIKER

Just exactly where have you taught before?

JOY STARR

Boy Meets World, Saved By the Bell,

**and Breaker High. And I wanna put
happy faces on your students, too!**

"And we want you to!" I whispered.

Pam made a weird growling noise between her
teeth. "This is *not* an audition!"

JOY STARR
You'd get a frowny face from me!

Then Joy (as I like to call her) dug into her large
shoulder bag. "So you can remember, here are
photos. . . ."

"Oh, I'll remember. . . ." My fingers shot out for
the photos, but Pam swung around and smacked
my hand.

"She's not getting the job! I'm in a contest! I
need help! Professional help!"

JOY STARR
(FROWNING) **You sure do, honey.
But I play teachers, not counselors.**

Then Joy slinked away across the stage and went
behind the curtains. The music stopped. She was
gone.

I cleared my throat. "I think Mr. Shell must have
sent her."

Miss Krabbiker humfed loudly. "Your producer is having a little joke with us, and it's not funny."

Principal Pangborn struggled to his feet. "Oh, dear, dear. I hope candidate number three is better."

I glanced at Pam. "Sure. I mean, how could it—like—get any worse?"

Tweeeee!

A shrill whistling sound erupted from the parking lot. We all ran out the front doors.

"Dude!" I said.

SCENE 7: PARKING LOT—SECONDS LATER

"Eight! Nine! It's like, can I stop now?"

"Five more, skinny!"

Booger Bob was doing push-ups on the sidewalk.

Leaning over him was a tough-looking coach sort of guy in a gray sweatsuit. He spun around when he saw us and spat out a whistle. He didn't look happy.

COACH-GUY

Push-ups, Pangborn! Laps, lady! Your school is in a crisis! I've never seen such wimps!

"Excuse me," the principal mumbled, "but who—"

COACH-GUY

Just a coach doing his job. You don't want your kids pinned to the mat, swimming downfield to graduation with two men out and dribbling without a helmet, do you? DO YOU?

"Well, no, I suppose not, but we don't need a—"

COACH-GUY

Okay. So first we throw out the desks and make each classroom into its own gym. Then we split into teams, boys against girls—

"But we need a *social studies teacher!*" Pam pleaded.

The coach-guy gave a puzzled look. "You mean *soccer* studies."

"No," Pam went on. "I mean, like—geography—"

"Jography?" He smiled. "Jogging's okay for girls—"

"Argkk!" Pam made a gargling sound and went for the guy. But before she could split him into teams, he leaped over the bike rack into a sports car. A moment later—*vrrmm!*—he screeched off in a cloud of smoke.

"Um, I'll just go now," Bob said. He ran away quickly.

Pam slapped her cheeks. "Ohhhh, my life is *over!*"

Then a softer voice spoke. "Excuse me? Principal?"

We all turned. In the cloud of exhaust clearing from the sports car stood a tall figure.

[MUSIC CUE: sudden angelic choirs singing]

Principal Pangborn squinted. "Who . . ."

"Yeah, who . . ." I said, also squinting.

But Pam and Miss Krabbiker pushed us both aside, as a man dressed in tweed and corduroy walked from the swirling mist. He seemed to come at us in slow motion.

The guy looked like David James Elliott of *JAG.*

Like David Duchovny of *The X-Files.*

Like David Hasselhoff of *Baywatch* (the early episodes).

I mean, the guy was perfect, all the way from his wavy hunk of sandy brown hair to the polish on his shoes. He even had chalk dust on his fingertips.

"Finally," Pam whispered. "A real teacher!"

The man held out a foot-thick wad of paper.

MR. PERFECT

Hi. Here's my resume. I've been a teacher for ten years. I love seventh grade. Social studies is my best subject. I can stay late for extra help. And my name is—

"David . . ." Miss K said as her eyes rolled up.

"You're . . . hired!" Pam blurted out.

SCENE 8: CAFETERIA—TUESDAY—LUNCH TIME

"So Pangborn actually hired him," Danny said as we sniffed our way to the cafeteria later that morning.

"Weird, huh?" I said. "The guy came out of a cloud of exhaust and he's perfect. The joke is, his name really is David. David Maggio. Mr. Maggio to us."

Now, I've always loved your basic TV eating scene. These seem to be favorite settings for sitcoms. I guess people like to watch other people sit at tables and talk.

But I doubt Leonard Shell liked cafeteria scenes. Aside from maybe a dropped tray or two, a slip on a banana peel, or someone coughing back the daily dried chicken special, there's not a lot of action.

But every now and then. . . .

When we entered the caf, Pam spotted us, leaped up from our usual table, stuck out her arms, and did that dance that looks like somebody stirring a cauldron.

"I'm gonna wi—in! I'm gonna wi—in!" she chanted.

I tossed my books on the table. "You and Joy Starr doing an act together?"

"Very funny." She twirled back into her seat. "My essay problem is solved. And . . . I'm gonna wi—in!"

At this point, Jay slid over to the table. "Hey."

I pointed to his face. "You know your chin is blue?"

"Dickens and Fenster are painting the inside of my locker," Jay said to me. "All that jelly from the first episode corroded the inside. It was a mess, Spencer."

I shuddered. "I was there, remember?"

Pam went on. "Mr. Maggio said we'd map out my whole project after class today. You know, when it works, life can be beautiful!"

"Speaking of beautiful," Danny said, "you people should have seen me last night. In my room. Me and my remote."

"Oh, that sounds cozy," said Jay.

Danny grinned. "Cable reruns. *Star Trek* and *Gilligan's Island.* Flick-flick-flick! Before you know it, Gilligan is beamed to the *Enterprise,* Spock is helping the Professor build that radio, and Ginger! She's lobbing coconuts at the Klingons! My brain was smoking. My thumb was flicking! Whole new way of watching TV!"

I gave him a squinty look. "Beaming back to

Earth for a second, Flicky, what's happening with you and Dee?"

"Eh," he said with a shrug. "After I waved yesterday, I think she sees me even less." He glanced longingly at the far side of the cafeteria.

[CUT TO: group of girls at another table]

Dee Weiden was holding court, surrounded by the most popular girls in the seventh grade.

"Maybe she'll notice your thumb," Jay said. "It's hard to miss that thing."

"Yeah," Danny said with pride, holding up the bulbous, mutant thing. "It sure is a beauty."

It wasn't. But Dee Weiden was. She looked like a girl from a teen clothes catalog. Danny had noticed this back in third grade. He had obsessed about her ever since.

"I love how she pushes her hair back," Danny said.

"Never happen," Jay said out of the corner of his mouth. He was chomping one of his mother's homemade salami and cheese grinders and glancing down at some pages of scribbled class notes.

Neither of which I'd *ever* seen him do before.

"What will never happen?" Danny asked.

"You and Dee. Never happen." Jay chomped again.

Danny frowned. "It could happen. Maybe."

"Is an asteroid coming?" Jay asked. "The big quake? Tidal wave from Japan? Then, maybe, if we're all gonna die, she won't cross the hall when she sees you coming. Otherwise, no." He wiped his mouth. "I know her type. She only sees people as popular as her."

Danny's frown got darker. "She talks to you, Pam."

"Because I'm popular," Pam said. "I only hang with you guys because . . ." She mumbled something and trailed off.

"Because you don't have great hair?" Jay asked.

I turned. "No, wait. This is good. Why *do* you hang with us, Pam?"

"Because . . . I don't know!" Pam snapped. "Maybe because you're funny."

"Funny?" I said. "You think we're funny."

"Looking. Funny-looking," she said. "Anyway, those people have no sense of humor. It's deadly at those tables. It's all patch-pocket jumpers and scoop necks and poly knits."

"The inner world!" Danny breathed. "Speak to me."

"I can't," she snarled. "I like funny. So sue me."

That's my Pam. That's why she's on my show.

"Listen, Danny," Jay went on, "I'm busy this week, but next week, I can give you some pointers.

Maybe we can do a whole show around me teaching you stuff.''

"I don't think so, Mr. D-Plus,'' Danny said. "I'll find a way to get Dee to notice me. I'll do . . . I'll do the flick.''

"The what?'' I asked.

"The flick, yeah. I'll flick myself from my show right onto Dee's show!''

That jarred me. "Your show? Since when do *you* have a show? I'm the one with the show. Even though you only watch half of it.''

[CUT TO: closeup of Danny's snorting face]

"Ha!'' he said. "Everybody has their own show, Spencer. Yours just has cameras, that's all.''

[CUT TO: closeup of Jay's smirking face]

"Except,'' Jay said, "Danny's show only has an audience of one.''

"Camera, back on me, please!'' I said.

[CUT TO: closeup of my face, where the camera should be]

"OH, YEAH?'' Danny fumed, bolting up from the table. "Well, I'm doing the flick. You'll see! You'll all see!''

He stormed out of the cafeteria, leaving his lunch tray.

Pam turned to Jay. "That was pretty harsh, but funny. But harsh. You sure know how to flick Danny's buttons."

"I only speak the truth," Jay said.

"Since when, Yoda?" I asked.

"Since I got a part on the Smart Show. Take a look at this quiz." Jay slid a sheet of paper across the table, picked up Danny's tray, and quietly left the cafeteria.

Pam and I looked at Jay's quiz.

Marked on the top was a big red A.

"Dude!" I mumbled.

SCENE 9: CLASSROOM—TUESDAY—FIFTH PERIOD

"This is going to be *soooo* perfect!"

Pam and I headed to Mr. Maggio's class for the first time. Actually, I headed. Pam skipped.

"You're not going to start dancing again, are you?"

"Perfect teacher. Perfect class. Perfect next two days. Leading all the way to my perfect essay!"

I gulped silently. Pam was very gleeful again.

We entered the classroom and took our seats. Out of the corner of my eye, I saw Chester "The Tank" Johnson ease into a nearby desk. He gave me a glance, then looked away. I wondered if he was mad that I hadn't done anything to make him mad this week.

"Per—*fect*," Pam repeated, as if I hadn't heard.

"Perfect is a strong word," I mumbled.

"The right word, Spencer," Pam said. "You'll see."

That was the second "you'll see" in two hours.

"You'll see" was usually trouble. Would it be trouble this time? We'll see.

Pam was so excited about this first Maggio class, she even broke into giggles with Dee Weiden, who took the seat next to her. Oh, those popular scoop-neck girls.

The cameras were humming from all angles. I knew Principal Pangborn was hoping for a good classroom scene on the show. We hadn't had a really good one yet—since you definitely could *not* count the scene in the first episode when Danny wore his nerd glasses in Miss Krabbiker's class and said a bad word he didn't know was bad until he got sent to the office. That was not good. That was the definition of a *not good* scene.

The red camera lights flickered on.

Camera pans around a typical classroom. Posters on the cinderblock walls. Bulletin board. Front and back chalkboards. Fluorescent lights on the ceiling. Four rows of six desks each, most occupied. We pan up through the rows, ending at the large gray teacher's desk in front.

Mr. Maggio was perched on a corner of his desk. He glanced around at us and picked up a thick book. He looked like a true teacher. He was sure dressed for it. Corduroy pants and nubby jacket with elbow patches.

MR. MAGGIO

Now then. Today, we'll be doing history.

Pam winked at me as she settled into her seat. "History. I'm doing a history essay. I'll get ideas. I'll win!"

I smiled back as the cameras moved into position.

MR. MAGGIO

I see by Mrs. Brady's notes that you were studying the American Revolution. Maybe we can start with a little question and answer.

He flipped through the book and stopped at a page.

MR. MAGGIO

Now, this looks interesting. I'm looking at a picture of two iron boats in a famous battle. What were their names?

The Tank's huge mitt shot up.

THE TANK

The *Titanic* and the Love Boat?

Mr. Maggio's thumb suddenly slid out of the pages and—*floop!*—he lost his place in the history book.

MR. MAGGIO
Ooops! Uh . . . I suppose I could go with that.

THE TANK
(PUNCHING THE AIR) **All right!**

"What?" Pam frowned at me. "Iron boats were in the Civil War. Not the Revolution—" Her hand shot up. "Um . . . Mr. Maggio, I'm not sure about all that. Can I use the encyclopedia?"

"Encyclopedia?" he said. "No, you can walk like everyone else."

Pam blinked for an instant. "Huh?"

I leaned toward her. "Maybe he's testing us?"

She shook it off. "Yeah, he's just getting started."

He *was* just getting started. He reopened the book.

MR. MAGGIO
Does anybody know where the Louisiana Purchase Agreement was signed? Ron, then Dee.

RON ZANKY
At the bottom?

DEE WEIDEN

Gettysburg?

MR. MAGGIO

Uh, no. That's where Abe Lincoln lived. You've heard of his Gettysburg Address. That means where he lived. It was the log cabin he was born in, which he built himself. Out of bricks.

Some of the kids giggled, but Pam seemed to suck all the energy in the room into herself. She went very quiet.

It got worse. For the next thirty minutes, Mr. Maggio flipped through the history book like Danny through the channels, mixing and matching all kinds of facts.

We learned—

—how somebody named John Wilkes had a booth at Henry Ford's Theater in Dallas when President McKinley was associated;

—how somebody called Frank Lynn invented electricity so that somebody else known as Eddie's son would have some place to plug his lightbulbs in;

—that Pearl Harbor was a famous jazz singer from Hawaii, and that Kitty Hawk was her sister;

—and finally that a guy named General Custard lost the stand for his uniform but people thought he said unicorn and they couldn't decide if it had a little or a big horn, but then he found the stand again and that's what is known as Custard's Lost Stand Found.

Through this whole whirlwind tour of bizarro American history Pam was growling and grumbling and fidgeting, until I thought she'd internally combust. Her eyes were growing to the size of those satellite dishes you see on people's roofs.

Finally, the teacher actually asked a question about the Revolutionary War. Pam pricked up her ears.

MR. MAGGIO
Who was the famous French general who helped us during the Revolution?

CHELSEA TURBIN
General Mills?

The Tank's paw again rose.

THE TANK
I see his name in the book, but I can't say it. I could write it on the board.

That took about three minutes.

THE TANK

L-A-F-A-Y-E-T-T-E.

Mr. Maggio blinked. "How the heck do you say that?"

THE TANK

Laf . . . at . . . feet?

MR. MAGGIO

Mmmm . . . possibly. . . .

I glanced over at Pam, thinking she was on the point of becoming her own personal nuclear device, when her hand shot up.

"Pam, don't do something you'll regret!" I whispered.

But the girl was beyond taking advice. Her eyes burned. Her cheeks were as red as the tip of her nose, which was somewhere redder than the ruby slippers.

"I know the answer," Pam said politely.

Mr. Maggio flicked his finger at her.

Pam stood up. Nobody ever stands in class.

Pam stood up. She looked the teacher right in the eye. And loudly, and clearly, and deliberately, she told everyone how to say the name.

"The French general's name is pronounced—"

MR. MAGGIO

Yes?

PAM

La . . . fart.

As she herself had done a few minutes before, the entire class now sucked in its breath and waited.

My heart stopped. I got cold. Then I got hot. Then my vision blurred. My forehead was a water-fall of sweat.

Mr. Maggio closed the book and rose from the desk.

MR. MAGGIO

You're . . . a troublemaker, aren't you?

PAM

Me? A troub— But you . . . I mean . . . those questions . . . those facts—

MR. MAGGIO

Dentertion for you.

Pam gave him a quizzical look, gave me the same, then turned back to him.

PAM

Do you mean . . . detention?

MR. MAGGIO

(SHRUGGING) **Whatever you call staying after.**

Pam sank back into her seat, stunned to silence.

Ron Zanky raised his hand. "Yo, Maggio? What's the homework? Mrs. Brady always wrote it on the board."

The teacher puffed his cheeks then blew out a long breath. "I don't know. Watch some TV. Let me know tomorrow what you saw, and you get an A. How's that?"

I confess, when the cheer went up—led by Dee and The Tank—I was sort of involved in it. I mean, I had so much other homework, not to mention trying to dodge Leonard Shell and his action agenda, I needed the break.

Besides, *Buffy* was on. She'd get me a free A.

But even while I cheered I felt a black hole of negativity spinning fast next to me. I turned, mid-hurray, to see the face of Pam, dark, scowling, and demonic.

Actually sort of like on *Buffy* when those creatures of the night hiss with that mutant face they have.

A millisecond before Pam exploded into vampire dust in her seat, the bell rang.

Brrnnng!

She blasted out of the room.

SCENE 10: HALL OUTSIDE MR. MAGGIO'S CLASSROOM—FOUR SECONDS LATER

"Get over here, sitcom boy!"

A hand grabbed my shirt and pulled hard as I left the class.

"Pam, don't hurt me!"

Her face was lobster-red with rage. "Where did you get this guy? Is he another dumb actor Leonard Shell sent over to make the show funny? Because, guess what, I don't think he's funny!"

I took a deep breath. "Calm down, Pam. You hired him, remember? I wanted Joy Starr."

She released my shirt.

I continued. "When he walked out of that cloud you got all gooey as if you were touched by an angel or something. Besides, Principal Pangborn thinks Mr. Maggio is the greatest thing since electric staplers. His resume is as thick as a phone book."

"It probably *is* a phone book!" Pam fumed. "This guy is not a teacher, he's a total fake! You heard him babbling in there. How is he going to help me win that essay contest? I need to win that dumb contest!"

I tried to think of something to calm her down. "At least we all get A's . . ."

Her eyes bugged out. "It's not about grades! I

mean—uck! This is going to sound really Pangborn, but my education is important to me. The teachers know that. Miss K, Mrs. Petrie, Mr. Kotter. We learn real stuff from them. But this guy! He's cheating us! I ought to . . ."

"Please don't! Here he comes."

Mr. Maggio walked out of the classroom.

Pam stepped forward. "Mr. Maggio?"

He turned. "Yo!" he said, just as Ron Zanky had.

Pam cleared her throat. "You gave me detention, remember?"

"Dentertion?"

"Right."

"Yeah, well, forget it. I don't have time."

"Oh. Um, thanks. You also said we could talk about the essay I have to do for Thursday, remember? The big essay contest?"

His eyes showed annoyance. "That again?"

"You were going to help me choose a topic and get me started and check my work. I'm running out of time. What topic should I choose?"

"I don't know. Do some dead guy. It's history, right?"

A blank look from Pam.

"So pick a dead guy, then write it or whatever, and I'll check it," Mr. Maggio said. "How's that?"

"But—"

"I gotta go."

Without another word the man walked away.

"That was weird," I said. "You think maybe Danny flicked us onto *The Outer Limits?*"

But then, just as I tensed up to take what I thought would be the inevitable whack on my arm, all anger slid from Pam's face.

Her lips, so tightly pursed just moments before, opened suddenly into a smile. I even saw teeth. She began scratching her nose, always a sign that her clever brain was hatching some plan.

"What are you doing?" I asked, afraid of the answer.

"Shh! Incoming idea."

"Should I duck?"

Pam breathed in quietly. "I know what I'm going to do. It's clear to me now. I'm going to bust him."

"Bust him? You mean like . . . what do you mean?"

"Spencer, I will do an essay that will totally nail Mr. Maggio *to the wall!*"

"No more walls. Remember last episode?"

But Pam wasn't there with me anymore. She had advanced to a higher plane. She now had a plan.

"You're not going to *win* this essay contest are you, Pam?"

The girl laughed wildly. "Spencer, I am going

down in flames! He's a fake teacher. And he's charming everybody in sight with his elbow patches and his fast A's. But he won't get away with it. Not with me around!"

I tried to smile. "Why do I think I'm not going to get away with it, either?"

"Because you're my friend. And friends stick together. Friends are nice to each other. Now, out of my way. I've gotta make somebody wish he was never born!"

I knew that—somehow—I was going to wish that, too. When I turned around I knew it for sure.

Principal Pangborn was leaping down the hall at me, wagging a videotape.

"Spencer!" he cried out, "It's horrible!"

"The pants?" I cried. "I can explain!"

"Spencer! WE HAVE A THIEF IN OUR SCHOOL!"

SCENE 11: AUDIO-VISUAL ROOM—
TUESDAY—LAST PERIOD

"A thief? In our school?"

I couldn't believe the words. Another plot twist!

I was still shaking when, a minute or two later, the principal and I stood before a bank of VCRs in the school's audio-visual room. He handed me the tape.

"One of your show's remote cameras captured this last night," he said in a hushed tone. "Now, Spencer, I don't have time to watch every single silly tape—"

Right, I thought. Then maybe he'd know how weird his new teacher was.

"—but maybe I should." He leaned in even closer. "Spencer, I think someone from your show is stealing!"

I gulped. I pushed the tape into a VCR.

SCENE: NURSE'S OFFICE—NIGHT

Camera pans across a medicine cabinet, a computer on a desk, a cot, a blue-and-white-striped pillow.

For what seemed like several minutes, the two of us just stared at the darkened nurse's office.

Suddenly, there is movement on the screen. A small hand reaches out of the shadows at the edge of the picture. It moves around, touching this and that.

"What is he going to steal?" I wondered aloud.

Finally, the hand reaches across the cot. Slowly, carefully, it grasps the blue-and-white-striped pillow. *Fwoot!* The pillow disappears.

FADE OUT.

"Did you see that?" the principal gasped.

"The pillow? It's not even a full-size pillow."

He shot me a look. "Stealing pillows is no joke, Spencer."

"No, sir." I cast my eyes downward.

"Crimes are being committed, Spencer. And because of your show, the whole nation is watching. Crimes lead to Jail . . . Spencer."

I didn't care for the way he said my name so close to bad upper-case words like Crime and Jail.

I knew I was innocent. I knew my friends were innocent. What reason could they have to steal a pillow? And the TV crew? They worked in television. Everyone who worked in television was rich!

But if all this was true, why did I feel so weird saying what I did?

ME

Nobody from my show is stealing stuff. Sir.

Principal Pangborn looked at me for a long time. "Good," he replied finally. "Because it could damage all we stand for at Preston Wodehouse Middle School."

I also didn't like that. It's always serious when a principal says the whole long name of your school.

"Here's the other part," he said, pointing back to the All Theft Video. "In the kitchen last night."

SCENE: KITCHEN—NIGHT

Camera shows light glinting off aluminum counters. A figure reaches under a counter, tugs at a cord.

The principal clucked his tongue. "Absolutely the *wrong* way to pull out a plug."

PERSON'S VOICE

(MUFFLED) Arg! Akkk! Out, darn plug!

Sloop! **The plug is out. The hands reach up and grasp a microwave. *Fwoot!* The microwave is gone.**

FADE OUT.

"And today is nachos!" the principal gasped. "How will we melt the special orange cheese dribbled on top?"

"Did somebody mention cheese?"

Suddenly, Jay was standing there behind us, gawking at the monitor. "Yeah, I heard about the tape. You know, I watch a lot of tapes. Maybe I can lend a hand."

Jay looked eagerly at me and Principal Pangborn. "You?" I said.

"The more help, the better," the principal said. "There have also been other things—big things—taken from the utility shed behind the school. You know we're keeping some equipment there while our workmen, Dickens and Fenster, are refitting the kitchen. I believe even one of our refrigerators is missing!"

"Wow," Jay gasped. Then he nudged his way past me. "Let's rewind. I think I noticed a clue." He hunched over the monitor. "I'll just press these buttons—"

"What are you doing?" I said. "That's not good for the machine. It's expensive."

But Jay wedged himself between me and the VCR. "Just getting a closer look at the hand on the screen."

"Yeah, I'll give you a hand," I said. "Will you move?"

"Each person in the world has different fingers."

"Right. If they didn't, they'd be the same person," I said. "Now please get out of the way!"

When I started to push him aside, Jay jammed his fingers—all his different fingers—at the VCR.

Hitting all the different buttons at the same time. Pause, Play, Fast Forward, Rewind, Eject.

The VCR must have felt like I feel when I'm talking to Pangborn and Shell at the same time.

Grrrr! The VCR gears and wheels started to grind inside the unit. The thing made a popping sound.

"That's not good," Principal Pangborn mumbled.
Kkk-kkkerrr-FLUNG!

A ragged ribbon of brown videotape erupted from the tape slot and slapped across the air toward me.

"Uh-oh . . ." Jay muttered. "Meltdown!"

"What the—" I cried. The snake of tape shot higher and higher, unreeling like a streamer.

Whumff! A puff of black smoke burst suddenly from the vents in the top of the machine.

"Did I do that?" Jay exclaimed.

"Well—duh!" I screamed, yanking out the cord. "You blew up the machine, you numbskull!"

Smoke drifted up toward the ceiling.

Smoke reached the sprinkler.

"Dear, dear, not the sprinkler!" the principal cried.

Yes, the sprinkler.

Before the principal could shut it off, the nozzle sizzled, spurted, and shot its spray down on Jay and me.

"Your stupid fingers!" I yelped as I sloshed after him.

"Yeah," he added, sprinting. "Thanks!"

SCENE 12: SCHOOL PARKING LOT—END OF DAY

School was over. Danny and I were on the front curb talking while we waited for our parents to pick us up. My mom was going to be late, which was good. I needed time to calm down and dry out. Do some clear thinking about things, if that was still possible.

"Truly bizarre," I said. "It's almost as if Jay ruined the tape on purpose."

"Could he actually *do* something on purpose?"

"It would be a new side of him," I admitted. "Thinking about something, then doing it."

"Instead of the other way around," Danny said. "Except for the thinking part. Which is not his specialty."

"He did get another A," I said. "His second today."

"Now that is truly bizarre."

It was a beautiful late afternoon. I took a deep breath of it and tried to collect my thoughts. "I'm glad Nurse Sternwood and her security guy couldn't identify us last night. I guess I pulled off my great disguise."

"You pulled off more than that!" Danny said. "Like your pants!"

I gave him the same evil eye I'd given Pam earlier. "Anyway, the SHARE program could have been totally ruined. Not to mention me and my show."

"Eh," he said. "Sternwood's probably too busy making up new rules to care. And I bet they found the lady who escaped. So don't worry. Take a look at this instead." He pulled out a flashlight and held it under his chin. He flicked the button with his thumb.

Flick. The light went on. "Spooky!"

Unflick. The light went off. "Not spooky."

Flick. "Spooky!"

Unflick. "Not spooky."

I stared at him. "It doesn't really work in daylight."

He shrugged. "It does build the thumb, though. Gotta be in shape by tomorrow night. *Celebrity Volleyball* versus *Killer Bees Attack!* Ouch, Spencer! It's New TV!"

I rolled my eyes. "Yeah, that's what it is. By the way, are you going to flick yourself onto Dee's show? We were all going to *see,* remember?"

He sighed like a tire losing air. "As much as I hate it, Jay's right."

"About each person having different fingers?"

"About me being unnoticeable. Dee Weiden

doesn't even see me. I have to do something different."

"Wear a sash? Use stilts? Ride a pony to school?"

"Something."

Poor Danny. I felt for him.

"I actually know what you're going through," I said. "For months I wanted this really cool mountain bike. But whenever I told my parents about it, it was like they didn't hear me, didn't see me. Drove me totally crazy."

He looked at me. "Is this story going somewhere?"

"Yes it is," I affirmed. "I soon realized why they phased out and wouldn't hear about that bike."

"Why?"

"They'd already bought it for my birthday! They just wanted it to be a surprise. Isn't that cool?"

Danny squinted at me. "You really don't know what I'm going through, do you?"

"Not a clue. But someday I hope to."

Danny grumbled for a while, then paused. "I wonder if Pam would help me. She knows Dee."

Errch! The main doors creaked open behind us.

"Someone's coming out!" I whispered.

It was Mr. Maggio. He didn't see us, but strode right through the side garden to the utility shed in back.

Don't Touch that Remote!

"Did that seem weird to you?" Danny asked.
"Just clomping his way through the flowers like
that?"
The doors creaked open again and Pam ran out.
"Like clowns from a circus car," I muttered.
"Which way did he go?" she asked us.
I pointed to the garden. "Follow his footprints."
"Uh, Pam," Danny said. "I was thinking. You
know Dee Weiden, right? Could you maybe talk to
her—"
"Later, Thumbsy. I'm hot on Maggio's case," she
said. "He's been sneaking around in very unteach-
erly places. I tried to tell Pangborn, but he just
points to Maggio's phone book resume. So it's up
to me. This guy can fool some of the kids all of the
time and all of the kids some of the time, but he
can never fool an honors-with-distinction kid any
time!"
"Except that you hired him," I said.
"He came out of a cloud!" Pam snarled. "The
exhaust fuzzed up my head. But never mind that.
He's heading around the back. I've got to go."
"Just don't commit any Crimes," I said in
upper case.
She smiled a knowing smile. "I'm curious. Curi-
osity in a student is called Research. Now, Danny,
give me your flashlight. I've got Research to do."

He gave it to her and she scurried around the school to the utility shed. The camerawoman was on her heels.

At that moment, Danny's father drove into the parking lot and Danny got in the car, jabbing that weird lumpy thumb high in the air. "See ya, Spenca!"

I waved as the Dompermobile pulled away. I was going to sit back down on the curb, wait for my mom, and try clearing my head again, when I smelled it.

Hot nacho cheese.

Coming from inside the school.

SCENE 13: SCHOOL HALLS—LATE AFTERNOON

The hallways were dark and empty when I entered the school. It was nearly suppertime, and only the janitors would be around. Maybe a teacher or two. I passed Principal Pangborn's office. Even he was gone.

Then, I heard something. Was it . . . humming?

I couldn't be sure. Empty, the school was much different than during the regular school day. The slightest sounds made things spookier.

Nnnnn. Yes, something was definitely humming.

I sniffed. Nacho cheese, definitely.

The creamy processed kind they use only in schools.

But the smell wasn't coming from the kitchen. The scent was stronger and the humming louder the farther away from the cafeteria I tiptoed. And I knew they hadn't replaced the stolen microwave yet.

Clearly, I was on the scent of the microwave thief!

I turned the corner into B wing. I started to wish I had Danny's exercise flashlight—which Pam was now flicking, for whatever weird purpose.

Then, suddenly, I didn't need a flashlight.

A strange orangey glow was coming from the end of the hallway. The pattern it cast on the floor was of a series of narrow strips of light.

As if the light were shining through . . . vents.

No! Dude! It couldn't be!

I crept down the hall. The humming got louder and—yes—the light was shining through vents.

The light was coming from *inside a locker!*

The remote cameras were taping me. I could see their little red lights flickering.

I edged up to the locker. Number 1243.

"What the—!" I gasped. "Jay's locker!"

I flashed back to our first episode when I watched this same locker oozing gobs of grape jelly crushed out from hundreds of tiny doughnuts. And now it smelled of spicy, stolen, humming, illegally heated cheese!

"Jay just doesn't get the locker thing!"

Bing! A tiny chime rang and the humming stopped.

I reached for the handle. I pulled on it.

"But how did he ever fit a microwave in here?"

WHAM!

Something flat and cold and sudden slammed into my forehead. Everything went black behind my eyes.

I faded out.

FADE OUT:

END OF ACT ONE

ACT TWO

FADE IN:
**SCENE 14: A SMALL ROOM—TUESDAY—4:30
P.M.**

When I faded back in, the cheesy smell was still
plugging my nose. I gazed out at a small room I
wasn't familiar with. "This isn't the nurse's office.
Where am I?"

"My locker," Jay said.

He was sitting at a round table three feet away,
leaning over a tremendous platter of nachos.

"Yeah, right," I said. "Where am I really?"

"The living room in my locker," he said. "Sorry,
my refrigerator is near the door. I was getting Cokes
when your head caught the fridge. You went
down, Spencer."

Living room? Refrigerator?

I focused and gazed again. The walls were a rich blue, like that smear of locker paint on Jay's chin earlier. The walls seemed made of metal. In fact, the room did look like the inside of a locker, only it was way too big.

"Either I shrank, or I'm having a wicked nightmare."

"Then the three of us are sharing it," Jay answered, gulping a Coke and crunching a cheesy chip.

"Three of us?" I said. "Who else is here?"

"Hey, kid, how's the head?"

I turned. I gulped. Sitting—reclining, actually—in one of those fat, couch-potato TV chairs wedged up behind Jay's table was Mr. Wiggins. Wiggy. He grinned at me from under his own huge plate of steaming nachos.

He moved his thumb, and the channel changed on a wide-screen television on the wall in front of him.

"Welcome to my house, Spencer," Wiggy said. "Pull up a seat." He nodded toward a stack of cafeteria chairs against the distant back wall. "We have nachos, we have cheddar popcorn, we have Triscuits. If you want, you can flick around the stations. I'm gonna check email."

"Uh, no thanks, I don't feel so—*you have email?*"

"It came with the cable hookup," Jay said, laying a math book on the table and cracking it open. "You see, it's not just my locker. I rented the two next door and the ones that back up on them. A hundred square feet."

"Rented?" I gulped. "You're doing real estate now?"

"I traded stuff to some sixth graders. They're happy."

I took a deep breath of cheesy air and sat up in the middle of what looked like a small condo. Tables, chairs, a rumbling air conditioner, bookshelves, a computer workstation, a refrigerator, a microwave.

"Lockers are for books, Jay. Backpacks. Jackets. Not doughnuts. Not furniture. Not cookware. And unless I missed a page in the school manual—*not people!*"

"But it's like the SHARE program. I'm sharing."

"What do you think SHARE stands for? Students Helping Aging Runaways Escape?"

"Spencer, that's good."

I looked my friend squarely in the eye. "Do you know how many laws you've broken here? Not to mention the stuff you've stolen! Is that a CD player?"

"I like to think of them as borrowed," Wiggy said.

"Right," Jay added. "Nothing has actually left the school. Stuff is just being rearranged."

"Rearranged!" I said. "Principal Pangborn is going to rearrange our heads! Jay, you've GOT A GUY LIVING IN YOUR LOCKER!"

Jay glared at me as if he were a genius and I was insane. "That's why I had to expand it, Pinky! Besides, you've been to Coconut Palms. Nurse Sternwood is bad news. I needed to get Wiggy out of that place!"

"And that's called kidnapping," I muttered.

"It was my idea," Wiggy said. "Sternwood runs her ship so tight, it squeezed the life out of me! So we came up with the laundry cart. Jay pushed, I escaped!"

"That's right," Jay said. "The same cart that I rescued you in, by the way. You should be grate-ful, Spencer."

While his email loaded up onto his computer, Wiggy disappeared to the back of the locker.

I wheeled around to Jay. "What the heck kind of monkey business are you running here?"

"I don't see any monkeys!"

"I see one!" I cried. "Look, I promised Principal Pangborn that no one from my show was stealing. And it's you! And all this construction! I mean—"

"Phh!" Jay waved off the accusation with one hand and held up a paper in the other. "Look, Spencer. B-plus. From Miss Krabbiker. And I did it fair and square."

"So? What does that have to do with—"

"Wiggy's been teaching me!" he said, popping another large, cheesy chip into his mouth. "Tutoring me. Before he came along, I thought Huckleberry Finn was a cartoon dog. I was Rufus the Doofus, Spence. But Wiggy knows everything. How else could I get these grades?"

I stared at Jay. "He's teaching you. Here in his office."

"Absolutely. You know I don't get good grades. Well, I'm getting them now. Thanks to Wiggy. Talk about Empowerment!"

I thought about it. "Okay, look, that's great. But you've got to find some other place for him. He can't stay here. And all this stuff has to go back."

"I'm not kicking him out of his house."

"It isn't a house!" I cried. "It's a locker! In a school!"

I heard a toilet flush from somewhere in the back

of the locker. I gasped. "You've got a bathroom in here?"

Clomp! Clomp! Clomp! I heard footsteps tramping somewhere above our heads.

"Pangborn!" I winced. "I told you!"

But it wasn't.

The short workman, Dickens, came down from somewhere in the ceiling, holding two coffee cups. "Fenster wants another cappuccino. I'd like a mocha with two-percent milk."

"Coming right up!" Jay said, turning to a giant silver coffee machine behind him. He flicked it on. "Spencer, how about you? Your mom won't be here for probably another ten minutes. Wanna cuppa somethin'?"

I gave him a face.

Dickens turned to me. "Jay's the man. Not like that nurse at the Villa. We did repairs there. Had to work twenty minutes straight. Which reminds me, we found bad plumbing upstairs. May take a day or two to fix."

"Uh-huh," I mumbled, squinting into the distance. "Is that . . . a ladder you came down? The ladder I fell off?"

"Just until we finish the staircase to the loft."

"The . . . loft?"

Jay chuckled. "Actually, the upstairs janitor

closet. It's where the inflatable futon and the bead curtain are going. Dickens busted through the ceiling for me.''

Busted.

Right. Just what I was going to be.

"Jay—" I started.

Shhhh! went the cappuccino maker.

I gave up.

I sank back onto the fluffy blue-and-white pillow from the nurse's office and wondered what kind of pillows they have in jail.

SCENE 15: MY ROOM AT HOME—TUESDAY EVENING

"Why are you sweating so much, Spencer? It's gross."

I opened my eyes to see Pam climb into my bedroom from the porch roof outside my window. She's been doing that since third grade.

I wiped my wet forehead. "I must have conked out after school. I had the worst dream."

"I know what you mean," Pam said, sitting herself in front of my TV. "I dreamt about Danny's thumb last night. Except that *he* was on the end of *it*. I woke up when the thumb asked Dee Weiden for a date."

"Humf," I humfed. "In mine, Jay had a guy living in his locker. They had all kinds of furniture and a loft—"

"Is that . . . cheese on your forehead?"

"Huh . . . ?"

"And you smell like . . . I don't know . . . cappuccino."

ME

Ahhhhhhhhhhhh!

"So, I guess it wasn't a dream?" Pam said calmly.
"Oh, my gosh!" I exclaimed, jumping out of bed.

"Jay has a locker the size of the Orange Bowl! And he stole stuff and he's got a little old man living in it! And they eat nachos all the time! And there's a bead curtain!"

"Speak to me, Spencer. I'm here for you."

I rattled off the whole horror story about the cheese and the microwave, making sure to describe every inch of the floor plan of Jay's double-decker executive locker suite. "Dozens of laws are being broken! And there's no end in sight. He's this far away from digging a pool!"

To all of this Pam listened calmly. Finally she said, "Old guy living in Jay's locker. That sounds about right. I have to say, Spencer, between Danny and Jay your show is turning into *The Twilight Zone*."

"Pangborn will go totally nuclear when he finds out."

"Maybe not." That's when Pam did her big wide Julia Roberts smile. "Our principal will be a little too busy busting Maggio to care about Jay's condo lifestyle."

"Meaning—"

"Meaning now I have evidence of Maggio fakery." Pam pulled a tape out of nowhere, slid it into my VCR, and hit Play. "This is what the camerawoman taped after I tracked our Mystery Man to the utility shed."

"The Teachers' Lounge isn't good enough for him?"

"He'd have to be a teacher. Which he ain't. Get the popcorn."

The screen flickered and showed the dark inside of the large storage shed behind the school. Pam's flashlight moved around like Dana Scully's.

SCENE: UTILITY SHED—TUESDAY AFTERNOON

Camera zooms in on Pam tiptoeing into the large shed. Before her is a bank of refrigerators with a gap that shows one refrigerator is missing. Maggio suddenly emerges from the shadows. Startled, Pam settles her flashlight on his face.

PAM

Oh, Mr. Maggio! What are you doing here?

MR. MAGGIO

I could ask you the same question.

PAM

I need to discuss the essay contest.

MR. MAGGIO

That dumb thing? Man, I hate this.

"Ouch!" I said. "Pangborn won't care for that."

PAM

At first, I was thinking of Benjamin Franklin. But I couldn't find much about him.

MR. MAGGIO

Because he died. No one remembers him.

I chuckled at that. Pam shushed me.

PAM

Oh, I get it. Then I thought the Civil War.

MR. MAGGIO

Wait until we know who won.

PAM

Then how about . . . George Washington? Would he be a good person for my essay?

MR. MAGGIO

(IMPATIENTLY) **Look, just do the essay, I'll**

93

read it, and we'll tell old Painbutt I
helped you. He'll never know the dif. Okay?

>   PAM
> (BARELY HIDING HER ANGER) Just what I
> had in mind. Bye.

>   MR. MAGGIO
> (TURNING AWAY) Sheesh!

Camera pulls back as Pam leaves.

>   **FADE OUT.**

The tape went snowy and Pam pressed Stop.

"Can you believe he called the principal that
name? Oh, this guy is bus—ted!" She grinned from
ear to ear.

"Just what you had in mind," I said, repeating
her phrase. "You are sneaky. But why George
Washington?"

"That's the genius part of my sneakiness, Pinky."

"Don't call me that."

"You see, Principal Pangborn loves Washington.
He knows everything about him. He even has
Washington's picture on his office wall. When I
read my essay, he'll know for sure what Maggio is."

"What is he, exactly?" I asked.

Pam breathed out hard. "I don't know. But one thing he's *not* is a teacher."

"Hey, guys!"

We turned to see Danny climb in the window. "I heard Maggio is giving A's for watching TV. You think if I tell him I'm watching double he'll give me two A's?"

"Kiss your A's goodbye," Pam said, wagging her head. "He's getting the boot when I prove he's a fake."

"Everybody loves him," said Danny. "If they knew you were going to cut off their supply—whew!"

Pam edged closer to him. "You won't tell them."

"I could be silent, for a price. . . ." Danny trailed off.

I nearly gasped. Pam actually did.

"For a price? For . . . Dee! You want me to introduce you to Dee! That's what this is all about, isn't it?"

Danny sighed. "Well, I mean, you *know* her. . . ."

"This stinks!" Pam cried. "It stinks bad. Like—"

"Old cheese?" I offered. "Half-rotten Spam?"

"Blackmail!" she said.

"Oh, come on," Danny pleaded. "I'm not going to say anything to anybody. But I'm desperate! I look at her, it's like I don't exist! I say something, she's deaf. I wave, she walks through me. It's like I'm some kind of ghost!"

"You'll be a ghost!" she snarled.

This needed the Spencer touch. "Pam . . ."

"And don't you *Pam* me!" she cried. She seemed ready to explode into a hundred pieces when, suddenly, she blew out a mouthful of air and did that trance thing she does when an idea threatens.

"Pam?" I tried again. "Everything okay?"

She broke from her trance and looked at Danny. "If you breathe a syllable of my plan to Dee, I will personally pull you inside out and make you swallow yourself!"

That remark blew Danny's hair back.

I pondered it, too. "Wouldn't that make him right-side-out again?"

"I promise," Danny said, giving Pam the thumbs-up.

[CUT TO: closeup of Danny's big, lumpy thumb]

The thing was bigger and uglier than ever.

"Oh, lovely," I said. "Does it have a fan club yet?"

"It's disgusting," said Pam, squinting at the lump. "Wait, is that . . . a *nose?* I think I see . . . lips!"

SCENE 16: SCHOOL STEPS—WEDNESDAY MORNING

"So, how did your big date go? Did you flick?"

"It wasn't a date."

Talk about weird conversations. I almost wished I was up on a ladder, a high ladder, so I wouldn't have to be a part of the conversation I had the following morning.

Danny The Flick rushed down the hall to me after second period on Wednesday. He and Pam and Dee had just finished math with Mrs. Petrie while I'd been in language arts with our home-room teacher, Mr. Kotter.

"Everything but a date," Danny said, shaking his head. "Pam went over to Dee after class, said, 'Here's Danny,' like she was saying . . . uh, I don't know . . . here's that telephone number for the . . . the . . . dumb place that nobody goes to or some . . . dumb . . . thing."

I blinked. "What?"

"Like something that doesn't mean anything!" he snapped. "That's how Pam introduced me. Then she bolted like she was . . . was . . ."

"Going somewhere?" I helped him.

"Yeah! Like that!"

"Then what?"

"Dee stood there, tapping her feet, as if she were waiting for a human to come along."

"Bad."

"Real bad. I had to go right to my best thing. I showed her the thumb. I said, 'Look at my thumb, Dee.' "

"Harsh," I said. "No chance for her to warm up to the concept of viewing a mutant being. Then what?"

"Then nothing. I told her about the flicking. More nothing. I was dying like a bad comedian. Like you when you tell jokes, like . . . like . . . somebody no good."

"Hey, I have my own show."

Danny sighed. "Please. This scene is about me, okay? So I tried to make small talk, but it's like I'm talking into a can."

"A can?" I said.

"Yes! A hollow thing that doesn't talk back! Nothing, she's saying nothing. She's ready to beam herself back to her girlfriends, when she just happens to open her mouth."

"She coughed?"

"No. . . ."

"She barfed?"

"No! Dee Weiden is the kind of girl who cannot barf! She is . . . well, she just can't!"

It took him a moment, but he calmed down again.

Then, with a look somewhere between guilty and delighted, he said, "She asked me if knew someone, because she wanted to meet him."

I scanned the brain. Ah, then I knew. "Me."

"No, Mr. Shell. She wanted to meet the producer."

"What?"

"I couldn't lie to her. If I'm going to be friends with Dee, I can't lie. So I said, sure. I tell you, Spencer, you should have been there. Her eyes lit up. She pushed her hair back with her hands the way she does. And—poof!—I was suddenly there. Taking up space in the hall outside math. Breathing air like a real person!"

"This isn't good . . ."

"Why isn't it good? I found Mr. Shell and introduced her. I had to, you know, talk to him. And, well, one thing led to another and out of nowhere, he starts listening to stuff I'm saying. Isn't that funny? Sort of?"

My heart stopped. He wouldn't have said those last five words unless something very unfunny was about to happen.

"You talked to Leonard Shell and he *listened* to you?"

"Not really."

My heart beat once. "So he's not insane."

"Actually, he listened to my thumb."

I clutched my chest. "There is a mouth on that thing!"

"Calm down," Danny said. "He asked me about the big lump. I couldn't lie."

"You could lie!"

"He was impressed with the whole flicking thing. He said it would help him focus about the show."

"Do you know what this means?"

"I'll get a credit on the show?"

"It means you *scared* him! Now he's going to make me do more and more dangerous action stuff. I'll probably get all kinds of hurt. I told you not to tell Mr. Shell about your thumb-dumb-dumb-DUMB-THUMB!"

Danny was quiet for a while. "It does explain why he got weird."

It was as if a chill breeze wafted across my legs. "How . . . how . . . weird?"

Danny frowned. "He said if everybody did the flick like I learned to do, we'd have no show. So he came up with the new idea."

My chilly knees got weak. My stomach rolled and heaved. My heart, forget that. It was dead.

"What new idea?" I squeaked.

Danny chewed his lip. "The one about the roof."

SCENE 17: ON THE SCHOOL ROOF—
WEDNESDAY P.M.

"You want me to fall off the school roof!"

"Not fall. Jump."

Leonard Shell, Danny, and I were up on the school roof. So was the entire crew, ready to tape a new scene.

"And not actually the roof," Mr. Shell said. "The *edge* of the roof." As if in some universe *edge* was better.

"I was talking to Danny and we agreed that our show needs *edge*. So, the *edge* of the roof. We're putting the *Edge* back in *Education*. Pangborn will like that, eh?"

"Oh, that's very funny," I said.

"Only sixteen feet high," Danny added helpfully.

"Sixteen feet!" I squeaked. "I've dangled from a window half that high and not liked it much. This'll be twice that much not fun!"

Danny blinked at that, then laughed nervously. "Oh, come on. Nobody's saying jump out of an airplane!"

"Out of an airplane. . . ." Mr. Shell repeated slowly, puffing on his cigar and suddenly looking off into the distance. "Right. No one's saying that yet. Besides, Spencer, you're protected. Look over the edge."

"*Look* over the edge?" I replied. "I can't even *think* over the edge." I leaned forward and glanced over anyway. On the ground below was a bulging square pad.

"A mattress? I'm supposed to land on that mattress?"

"You will if you aim for it," Mr. Shell said.

But even as I stared at my life-saving mattress, it began to slide away into the bushes. "What the—"

Then I saw a pair of hands in the bushes, pulling it in. A pair of hands with all different fingers.

It was Jay! And he was stealing my safety mattress!

"Hey, bring that back—" I yelled.

"Ah . . . ah . . . Spencer?"

I froze. Principal Pangborn was hustling across the roof huffing at me! In a fraction of a second, he would be at my side. He would look down to see Jay dragging that mattress (which was stealing) across the bushes (damaging school property) into the main hallway (when Jay should be in home room) and into his locker (whoa!). How many crimes was that?

"Spencer," the principal said. "I want to be certain nothing goes wrong, and that you don't hurt yourself."

"I don't have to," I said. "My friends do it for me."

Principal Pangborn chuckled. "Yes . . . yes . . . what?"

At least Wiggy wasn't up there to complicate matters.

Doy! Totally on cue, Wiggy came trotting across the roof behind the principal's back. We must have disturbed his tanning session. The principal started to turn.

"Agkkk!" I shrieked. Then I began to babble.

ME

George Washington is terrific!

"Er . . . excuse me? George Wash—"

ME

But you don't want to be like Washington when it comes to grades. No way! You don't want to go down in history! Ha-ha.

I hoped by shouting something about Washington, I would distract the principal so Wiggy could shoot down the stairs without attracting attention. Which he would have done. Easily.

Except for the cheese.

SCENE 18: SECOND-FLOOR STAIRS AND HALL—MOMENTS LATER

Cheese was in the air.

Actually, it was on the stairs leading down from the roof. Orange cheese had obviously dripped off Wiggy's stupid nachos, which he'd been carrying yet another stupid platter of!

The principal's nose jerked up suddenly and twitched as Wiggy disappeared down the stairs. "Does anyone else smell that? Do you smell cheese, Spencer?"

"Cheese . . . as in what, sir?" I said.

"It's coming from here!" he said, hustling toward the roof stairs. "Where there's cheese, there's our microwave. Where's there's a microwave, there's our thief!"

My life was melting all around me. But it didn't smell like cheese.

"There's a scent of Spam coming from the gym, sir! Let's go there!" I leaped back from the roof's edge.

But the principal's ears weren't working. His nose was. It poked down the stairs and the rest of him followed it. "My wife, Carmen, makes excellent nachos, you know. . . ."

[CUT TO: second-floor hall]

Following one drip after another, the principal sniffed his way down the main upstairs hall all the way to the door of the janitor's closet. I realized in an instant that Wiggy must have escaped into Jay's loft.

"Dead end!" I shouted. "Oh, well. Let's go to the gym and hunt down that nifty Spam. Mmm-mmm!"

Pangborn shook his head. "No, Spencer. We must clean this mess. Luckily, here is the janitor's closet."

"I'll do it!" I cried.

Too late. The man flung the door open and lunged in for where he thought the janitor's mop should be.

Not knowing that the mop—and the floor—had been rearranged. Oh, it wasn't pretty.

[CUT TO: Pangborn entering closet]

"Aghkk!"

He slipped off the top step of the loft staircase, was flung down onto his back, and ka-thumped from one step to another—*thump! thump! thump!*—all the way down to the main level, at which point he somersaulted over the back of Jay's sofa and onto the mattress I was supposed to fall on and that Jay must have just stuffed through his locker door.

Unfortunately, the principal's weight was all on one side of the mattress, so he slid—gently—right under the table where Jay and Wiggy were now sharing nachos over a copy of *Tom Sawyer,* which they seemed intensely into.

"Hi," said Jay, absentmindedly, when he and Wiggy glanced over at Pangborn. All six eyes met.

"Jay?" Pangborn sputtered. "Who—what—where?"

It was then that Genius Jay realized the principal was a surprise guest, could get him totally suspended, and maybe even jailed, so he reacted in a typical Jay way.

He panicked. "NOOOOO!"

Jay leaped up wildly, feet flying, elbows jerking back into the CD player, which jammed between two CDs, causing it to blow out suddenly with a noise like anvils dropping into an empty Dumpster.

JUNG-JUNG-JUNG-JUNG-JUNG!

The sudden impact of sound jolted the principal to his feet and—somehow—sent him lurching and spinning quickly across the small room toward Jay's locker door.

It was then, I think, that I got the brilliant inspiration to get downstairs as soon as possible.

"OUT OF MY WAY!" I shrieked. Then I tore off from the janitor's closet on the second floor, jumped down the side stairs, and raced along the first-floor hall to Jay's locker in a record-shattering 9.3 seconds.

[CUT TO: me, skittering down to locker 1243]

I threw open Jay's locker at the exact moment Principal Pangborn hurtled out of it, still spinning wildly, but now starting to make noises. "Wuh, wuh, wuh . . ."

Jay himself was in midair, his fingers gripping a cheesy nacho, trying to leap over the principal and out into the hall in a single bound.

He fell short, slammed into the rearranged stack of janitor mops, and launched himself out the door, the mop draped over his head like a very bad wig.

Pangborn, completely dazed and wobbling on his feet, glanced at Jay and his lips curled into a weird grin.

"Wuh, wuh, wuh, why Carmen! You're looking a little like George Washington today. . . . "

Jay, with unknown presence of mind, offered the principal his last nacho. "Eat your cheese . . . dear."

"Mmm. . . . " Pangborn's eyes rolled up into his head.

I shut the locker door and twirled behind him to keep his head from hitting the linoleum. Only to realize too late that one of my pant cuffs was caught in a hinge.

[SOUND EFFECTS: **sound of ripping cloth: *KRRIPPPP!***]

Instant giggling.

I turned to see Dee Weiden and the usual pack of super-popular girls standing near the water fountain.

Murmuring of cheese, our principal sank to the floor.

Feeling a draft on my legs, I ran.

SCENE 19: OUTSIDE MY HOUSE—
WEDNESDAY EVENING

By the time Principal Pangborn began to recover some bits of disjointed memory, school was over.

I tore home, hoping he wouldn't call my parents, found out he hadn't yet, then tied up the phone for the next two hours calling Pam, Jay, and Danny and telling them to meet me.

The moment I hung up, however—

Brrnng! The phone rang.

I started to run.

Brrnng!

"It's probably for you, Spencer!" my father called.

Brrnng!

"Let the machine get it!" I yelled.

Brr—

Too late! Someone picked up. I started running faster.

"Spencer, honey!" my mom called. "It's Mr. Shell. He's talking about airplanes—"

"Akkk!" I slammed out the screen door, ran across the patio and down the street along the neighbor's yard.

I didn't stop until I reached the big palm tree near the sidewalk. Grabbing its trunk, I slid around to the far side, slumped against it, and tried to catch my breath.

Not easy to do, given the way things stood.

Pam The Detective was after Mr. Maggio, while Danny The Flick was after Dee and got Mr. Shell to go after me. Meanwhile, Jay stole a guy from Coconut Palms, threatening to blow the SHARE program wide open, not to mention that Jay and his pal Wiggy were snatching appliances and bedding and busily scarfing nachos in a totally illegal condo centrally located in our school!

While all these thoughts spun in my head like maniac airplanes, I realized at once what we needed to do.

Jay and Danny were the first to arrive. Before Jay even opened his mouth, I started in.

"We have to get Wiggy back to Coconut Palms—"

"It's worse than that, Spencer!" he broke in. "We have to get Wiggy back to Coconut Palms!"

I stared at him. "Isn't that what I just said?"

"But now there's going to be a bedcheck!" Jay said with panic in his eyes.

"A bedcheck?" I said. "What's a bedcheck?"

"Where they check the beds to see if everybody's there," said another voice. Jay stepped aside and suddenly Wiggy was there.

He had been standing behind Jay the whole time.

Wiggy continued. "Mrs. Burke emailed me. If I'm not in my bed by tomorrow, they'll say I ran away. Nurse Sternwood will blame Dr. Goodwin, there will be a scandal, and Sternwood will take control of the Villa!"

That took me a minute. Then it hit me.

[CUT TO: my face, in shock!]

"THAT'S JUST EVIL!" I shrieked in all upper case.

"That's about the size of it," Wiggy said.

Jay tapped my shoulder. "Not only that. If Wiggy isn't back, they'll start a manhunt. He'll be found in the school. We'll all be busted."

"Busted?" said a voice behind us. "I love that word!"

Pam trotted up the sidewalk. "Especially when I'm doing the busting. And I'm getting closer all the time."

"Well, that cop is getting closer to me all the time."

We all turned to Wiggy, who had said that.

"Cop?" Danny said. "What cop?"

"Did the principal call the police about those thefts?" I asked. "Because . . . Jay did it! Jay did it!"

"No, no, no." Wiggy shook his head. "I'm talking about the head of security at Coconut Palms."

We continued to stare at the little old guy.

I recalled how the shadowy security guy chased me all around the Villa shouting into his walkie-talkie. "I never saw his face. What about him?"

"I think he saw me when I was tanning on the roof."

More staring at Wiggy.

"The school roof?" Danny said.

"Uh-huh."

"Let me get this straight," I said. "The head of security is at *our* school?"

Wiggy nodded. "He's pretending to be a teacher."

At this point, Pam sucked in about a gallon of air. Then she exploded. "MAGGIO!"

She practically punched a hole through my arm. "I knew it! I knew it! I knew it! Mr. Maggio is from the nursing home! He is *such* a fake!"

"He's a real security cop," Wiggy added. "Nurse Sternwood must have sent him to find me."

"Whoa!" I exclaimed finally. "Maggio is the security guy from the nursing home? That explains everything! Why he doesn't know his Revolution from his Civil War, why he won't help Pam with her essay, why he's always sneaking around!"

"Why his shoes are so shiny," Danny added. "Teachers' shoes are way more beat up."

"Yes, yes, yes!" Pam went on. "At the beginning he poured on the charm like a cheap aftershave. But when his aftershave ran out, he stank!"

"Wow, Pam," Jay gasped. "That's poetry."

"Busting him will be poetry, too," she said.

"Wait," I said. "*You're* going to bust *him?* No, he's going to bust *us!* And the school! Don't you get it? He's not just a bogus teacher, he's a security guy. He's like a policeman. You know what the SHARE program means to Principal Pangborn. If Maggio blows the whistle on Wiggy and us, everything explodes!"

"This is *sooo* perfect," said Pam in a very calm way.

I turned to her. "HOW CAN YOU BE SO CALM!"

"Because I see the big picture," she replied. "If you try to get Wiggy back tonight, Maggio will be there waiting for you. He'll nab you. I mean, he already suspects that Wiggy's here. But he needs proof. By tomorrow night, it'll be too late."

"Why tomorrow night?" Danny asked.

"Because our favorite fake teacher will be at school sitting next to me for the essay contest. When I blow his cover, he'll be in trouble for im-

personating a teacher. Plus, while he's at the con-
test, security at the home will be at its weakest.
Tomorrow night is when you break in. And once
Wiggy's back in his bed—"

"His *real* bed!" I added, casting a harsh look
at Jay.

"—there will be no evidence for anyone to
find."

I thought about that. "What about Jay's sky-
scraper in the middle of school? When Principal
Pangborn remembers all the gruesome details about
his tumble today, he'll nail us but good."

Pam shrugged in her easy way. "Dickens and
Fenster built it. They can unbuild it."

We all looked at Pam. Her smile was growing.
"Besides," she said. "When Dr. Goodwin returns—
and a quick call from me to Mrs. Brady will make
sure she does—Maggio and that bogus nurse will
get what's coming to them."

"But will it work?" I asked. "It can't. No way.
Can it?"

"Sure," Pam said, then she laughed. "It's so
funny when you think about it. Maggio used up all
his teacher lines to get the job. Then he started
making them up."

"Like me in Spanish!" Jay said. "I can say 'where
are the meatballs?' *Donde están las albóndigas?* But

that's pretty much it. Unless the meatballs are lost or missing, I've got nothing to say.''

I sighed deeply, wiping my sweaty forehead. ''You're out of luck, Jay. I'm pretty sure the meatballs are right here.''

He looked around. ''Where?''

Pam tapped my shoulder. ''Spencer, you know there's a big bonus for you in this whole thing.''

''Parole when I reach eighteen?''

She shook her head. ''No. Mr. Shell will love a break-in. He'll eat it up. That's action!''

''Vrrmm?'' I said.

SCENE 20: IN SCHOOL—THURSDAY

Thursday was a living nightmare. I grew old waiting for it to pass.

Every class I took—science, math, language arts, Spanish, reading—I kept waiting for the Wiggy time bomb to go off. Every time I hit the halls, I expected to see Pangborn wagging a videotape at me. Or Maggio leaping out of nowhere waving a pair of handcuffs.

It was tough navigating from one class to the next without passing either the first- or second-floor entrances to Jay's locker.

[CUT TO: me, skulking out of class]
[CUT TO: me, scrambling down the hall]
[CUT TO: me, hiding behind bigger kids]

And Wiggy? It was no wonder he and Jay hit it off. When Jay grows up—if Jay grows up—he'll probably be just like Wiggy is.

In the great spirit of Education, I suppose I shouldn't have complained. Wiggy was one guy who didn't have an Empowerment problem.

And in his bizarro way, he was actually good for Jay. He was a teacher. A real teacher. Thursday second period, Jay reeled in another B-plus, this time in Spanish.

I guessed he found the meatballs.

By the time the final bell rang and everybody left the building, I was worn out. I trotted from my own locker—where I kept normal stuff, like books and Joy Starr's pictures—over to Jay's.

The guys and I had agreed to meet there.

To plot the Big Break-In.

SCENE 21: JAY'S LOCKER—THURSDAY AFTERNOON

"Welcome to Pee Wee Freeman's Playhouse," I said.

"This is gorgeous," Pam exclaimed, when we all gathered in Jay's locker living room. "I heard there's a bead curtain? I love bead curtains. Very Pier One."

After a short tour for Pam and Danny, and for me of the second floor, which was a sort of penthouse for weirdos, we called our parents from Jay's cell phone and told them we were staying for the Big Night.

Then we got right down to business.

Danny had a plan. A scientific plan. He said he'd seen it on TV once, which normally would have been good enough for me, except for the Phase One part of the plan.

"Bring some string," he said. "That's all we need."

I looked at him. "String?"

"String," he repeated. "It's a prop for Phase One of my plan. You know what string is."

"The stuff inside yo-yos?"

"Right," Danny said. "We bring a ball of string with us to the Villa."

"And what?" I said. "Jump rope for Sternwood?"

"Not rope," Danny said sharply. "String."

"Are you sure you saw this on TV?" Pam asked.

"That's why I know it will work," Danny replied. "Television is a very educational . . . uh . . . thing."

"That's good enough for me," Wiggy said.

"I don't know . . ." I said.

"If I may continue," Danny said, as if he were the master planner from some caper movie. "Take the string and find a big tree that touches the building."

"There's one at the entrance," Wiggy said helpfully.

"Good," Danny continued. "Someone then climbs the tree and ties the string to a bunch of those loose roof tiles that adorn the roof."

"Adorn?"

"That was the word they used on TV," Danny said, with a look toward me. "Then our climber climbs down and pulls the string. The tiles crash to the ground, the guards are distracted, and we sneak into the building."

"Did Mr. Shell give you this idea?" I asked.

"Actually, I saw it on *ER Cops*," Danny said.

I threw my hands up. "Terrific! It's not bad

enough we're breaking into a nursing home, but we also have to steal ideas from another show!"

"Do you have a better plan?" Jay asked.

"Two minutes," I scoffed confidently. "I'll think one up in two minutes."

Three hours and nineteen minutes later I was still crouched on the floor with my head in my hands. Everybody started to poke me. Fifty-eight minutes after that, when the official school clock on the wall of Jay's loft struck seven PM, and I still hadn't come up with anything, I reluctantly accepted Danny's plan. We broke our huddle. It was time to go.

First stop, get Pam to the courtyard.

For the Big Essay Contest.

SCENE 22: SCHOOL COURTYARD—EARLY EVENING

The school's central courtyard was like an oversize patio, big flagstones on the ground, and surrounded on three sides by low walls. If you saw our first episode you know this is where Jay caught the flying doughnuts.

In front of the far wall was a podium and three rows of chairs facing out. This was the stage.

Principal Pangborn was there with Mrs. Pangborn, who didn't look a bit like the father of our country. Miss Krabbiker sat next to her, and Mr. Maggio next to Miss K. An empty seat next to him was for his prize student.

Pam Scott. The dentertion girl.

Other teachers and their prize students from different schools were arranged in other seats behind the podium.

Dozens of chairs facing the stage were starting to fill up with parents and kids. The evening air was warm and nice. All in all, it was a beautiful showcase for Pam.

She edged out. "The next explosion you hear will be my essay going down in flames."

"Lose good," I said.

"Bomb well," Danny added.

"Fail for us," said Jay.

Pam smiled at all of us. "Thanks. I'll do my worst."

Just before she went to her seat, Ron Zanky, Chelsea Turbin, The Tank, and a bunch of other kids from Mr. Maggio's class filed into the very last row of chairs.

At once, they began to pass a paper bag among them, each one reaching in and taking something out.

"I don't like the look of that," I said, looking back to see where the bag started. "Dee Weiden!" I gasped.

"Oh," Danny said. "Ha . . . about that . . ."

Pam turned to him. "What?"

"Well . . . uh . . . you'll think this is funny."

"Go ahead," Pam said. "Make me laugh."

"Well, um, I saw Dee again after fourth period and, you know, she started to not notice me again."

"I can see it happening," Pam said, edging closer.

"So I sort of mentioned, I mean, I guess I told her—"

"Told her . . ."

"Your plan to expose the fake teacher."

There was a blur in the air as Pam flew at Danny's unprotected head. "You're Spam, Domper!"

I think she would have done that turning inside-out thing, followed by the self-swallowing thing, if Jay hadn't pulled her back. "They're starting!" he yelped.

Pam eased up and burned a hole through Danny with her eyes. "I'll get you, Flicky Boy! And your little thumb, too!" She scrambled away into the courtyard.

When she took her seat, Principal Pangborn rose and went to the podium.

PRINCIPAL PANGBORN
Now, then. I am pleased to open this year's Citywide Student Essay Contest with the entry from our school. Pam Scott is one of our finest students. And Mr. Maggio is one of our finest new teachers!

THE KIDS IN THE BACK ROW
YAAAAAAAAY, Mr. Maggio!

I guessed that the principal still hadn't seen this week's tapes. I made a mental note that keeping tapes from him would probably turn out to be a good policy.

PRINCIPAL PANGBORN

**Miss Scott and Mr. Maggio have
worked extensively together. Now
they will honor Preston Wodehouse
Middle School with their entry.**

The courtyard chimed in with a round of applause. Pam went to the podium, clacked her papers on it, looked back at Principal Pangborn—whose smile could not have been bigger—and then looked out at her audience.

PAM

**This essay is dedicated to Mr. Maggio,
who helped me check every fact.**

She smiled at the fake teacher. He managed a sort of who-cares smile back, while his eyes darted around. Probably looking for Wiggy.

There was a slight rustle of paper bag from the back row. Then Pam cleared her throat and began to read.

PAM

**In his later years, George Washington
lived at Mount Vernon. Mount
Vernon is Italian, meaning "The Horse**

of Vernon" or "Vernon's Horse."
Because a mount is a horse.

PRINCIPAL PANGBORN
(TILTING HIS HEAD) What was that?

PAM
Now, we don't know who this Vernon
person was or what kind of horse he
had, but Washington really seemed to
want it.

"Oooh, I smell something burning," Jay said.
"The air smells like peaches to me," I whispered.
"Funny, I smell Spam," said Danny. "Let's go."

SCENE 23: COCONUT PALMS REST VILLA— EVENING

"Did you ever notice the way some doors swing out and others swing in?"

"Climb the tree, Spencer."

"Yeah, but sometimes you push the door because it looks like the pushing kind, but really it's the pulling kind and then you feel silly and people are looking—"

"Climb the tree."

Right. The tree.

It was a decent enough climbing tree, branches every few feet, lots of leaf coverage to hide me. All in all, a good tree. Except it was three stories high.

After cutting through some backyards, one baseball field, two streams, and a parking lot, the five of us—me, Danny, Jay, Wiggy, and the camerawoman—arrived at the entrance to Coconut Palms, where we waited in the bushes.

The camerawoman had been busy hooking up a portable monitor to show us what was happening at school.

And I had been jabbering small talk to keep from going one-on-one with the tree. But now I had to face it.

"String," Danny said, thrusting a wad into my hand.

"Why don't *you* climb the tree?" I said to Danny, suddenly thinking up a great alternative plan.

Danny grinned. "I have to carry my flashlight."

"Why can't I carry the flashlight?" I asked.

"Because it's *my* flashlight!"

I winced. "But I still hurt from the ladder and the refrigerator and the wedgie. I don't wanna climb!"

Jay shrugged. "Well, I'm Wiggy's SHARE partner. My place is with him."

I turned finally to the camerawoman. "Will you catch me if I fall?"

"I'll catch the action," she said, tapping her camera.

With a harsh look at everyone, I stuffed the string in my pocket and began to climb. Hand over hand, foot over foot I went. Amazingly, I did not fall to my death.

Near the highest branches, the tree grazed the roof directly over the Villa's main entrance.

I groped for a loose tile. They were cemented solid!

"What the—!" Then it hit me. "Dickens and Fenster!"

Of course! They had fixed the tiles! They were

doing repairs here just before I saw them in Jay's locker!

I pounded the tiles with the heel of my hand. As if there was some other part of me I could hurt, I nearly broke my wrist. Finally—*crrrk!*—some tiles came loose. Wrapping the string around a bunch of them tightly, I dragged them over to the edge of the roof and balanced them there.

The whole thing took about fifteen minutes.

I dangled the string down, took a deep breath, then slowly made my way down the tree.

Amazingly again, I touched earth with my feet first.

"This," I proclaimed with a huge grin, "is the beginning of a new era. The era of foolproof, no-hitch plans!"

I took a deep breath, and as I prepared to yank the string and enter Phase Two of the plan, I happened to catch a glance at the camerawoman's portable monitor.

[CUT TO: school courtyard]

Judging by the position of Principal Pangborn's furry eyebrows, which had fused into a single hedge over his red nose, things weren't going well back at the ranch.

PAM

Over the years the word horse became house, because Washington wanted to live there. He didn't want to live in a horse, because it was smelly and pretty cramped even inside a large horse. . . .

It was way too painful. I pulled the string. The evening silence was shattered.

[CUT BACK TO: Coconut Palms Rest Villa]

CRASH!

The tiles exploded on the front walk with a sound like a small nuclear device going off. It did the trick.

The double front doors blasted open, and our two burly friends, along with the desk nurse, rushed out onto the front lawn.

"Get the repair guys, stat!" one of them grunted, gazing up at the roof. As quickly and quietly as we could, all five of us slipped from behind the bushes and rushed into the entrance before anyone saw us.

"Like a dream," I whispered. "Now—Phase Two!"

We headed down the empty hall for the stairway up to Wiggy's room. Then I took a moment to glance once again at the monitor to see how Pam was doing.

Ouch!

[CUT TO: school courtyard]

PAM

But the weird part is that Washington's house was not even in Washington, but in Virginia. Which is not the same as Vernon, even though both words begin with V. Another weird part is that the very next letter after V in the alphabet is . . . what?

ALMOST EVERYBODY

W!

PAM

For who?

EVERYBODY

Washington!

Principal Pangborn jumped to his feet and started huffing. "Ah . . . ah . . . Pam?"

But we had our own development.

"I'm hungry."

"What?"

[CUT BACK TO: Coconut Palms Rest Villa]

"I'm hungry!" Wiggy growled as we climbed the stairs and onto his floor. "It's past suppertime and they'll lock the kitchen soon. You know Sternwood's rule number one. I'll starve before morning. Bad food is better than no food!"

"What! What?" I choked. "What about the bed-check! What about the reason we're here?"

But the old guy was already gone.

"I'd better go after him," Jay said. "He's my guy. Besides, all this tree climbing has made me hungry, too!"

I glared at Jay. "I was the one in the tree!"

"But my heart was up there with you, and it's hungry!" Now Jay was gone, too.

"I can't believe this!" Danny snarled.

"Numbskulls!" I grunted. "We'd better follow them."

But before we could, one of the patients' doors flew open. Poor Danny. He never had a chance.

"It's Danny The Flick!" Mrs. Burke cried, wheeling into the hall. With her were about a dozen patients.

"Teach us that thumb thing!" one shouted.

"You promised to share!" another called out.

"It's great therapy!" yelled a third. "Flick! Flick!"

"But we're on a mission!" I pleaded.

No good. They pounced on Danny like a herd of tigers. His expression when he realized what was happening will be etched on my mind forever.

Danny, however, was nearly etched on the nearest wall forever. I tried to grab him away.

"Spencer, help!" he cried. "Flick me off this show!"

Glup! An oozy sort of slapping sound muffled what would have been Danny's cheese-curdling scream.

I recognized his thumb jutting out from under some lady's arm. I began tugging on it. Danny slid to the floor like a damp towel. I had to get him out of there. Drool was dribbling down in gobs from his lower lip. Shock was setting in. I dragged him away.

"But his thumb and his cheeks belong to the world," Mrs. Burke said. "We're his greatest fans!"

"No!" I cried. "Stay away. He has . . . the plague!"

I yanked him to safety down the hall. When his eyes rolled up into his head, I went into high gear.

"Danny! Danny!" I said sharply. "Don't leave

us! Back away from the bright light! Danny, you're at the beach.''

"The beach?" he repeated. "The Baywatch beach?"

"Uh-huh. With Dee Weiden. . . ."

"Dee? Hi, Dee."

"She's pushing her hair back that way she does."

"Oh, whoa!" Danny muttered.

"You're going to be okay, Danny," I assured him, as we headed down the hall. "You're going to make it."

"With Dee?"

I couldn't promise that. But I couldn't break the spell.

"We'll see. . . ."

We hit the corner and I peeked down a new hallway. It was empty except for a woman in a suit standing before a closet. She reached in, took out a blue uniform, and unfolded it. It was a long doctor's coat.

Danny shook his head as if he were shaking water from his ears, then he perked up. "Is that Dee?"

I grinned. "No, a doctor. And she's got—disguises."

When the hall was empty, we snuck down to the

closet, yanked the door open, and dived in. We pulled blue shirts and pants over our clothes.

"We better not run into Sternwood," Danny said.

"Or if we do run into her, it's hard enough so she falls over and we can escape," I said. "Let's put some surgical masks on."

Danny pulled two masks down from the shelf and gave me one. "You know, I'm sort of getting into this action stuff."

I snorted. "Just as long as we get out of it okay."

We reentered the hall, looking pretty much like doctors. Well, short doctors.

"We need to look busy, too." Danny pointed to a rolling cart of covered aluminum pans.

"Supper leftovers?"

"Exactly." He nodded behind his mask. "We carry these food pans back to the kitchen, find Wiggy, and escort him to his room before High Commander Sternwood gets there with her mighty clipboard."

"Excellent," I said. "It might actually work."

Danny picked up the covered pans. "These leftovers smell terrible. No wonder Wiggy complains so much."

I thought about how great things were going for

us. That made me wonder how Pam was doing at school. . . .

[CUT BACK TO: school courtyard]

PAM

Horses live in stables, but Washington wanted tables rather than stables. Otherwise all his food would fall on the floor. I mean, have you ever had dirt in your food?

The principal began waving his arms.

PRINCIPAL PANGBORN
No! No! No!

"Khhh!" It sounded like Darth Vader with asthma. "What?" I said.

[CUT BACK TO: Coconut Palms Rest Villa]

"Khhh!" Danny breathed again behind his mask. He slapped me on the shoulder. "Luke, I am your father!"

"Who?" said a voice behind us. We turned.

Nurse Sternwood stormed over to us, staring at us with her dark eyes, and sending shivers up my spine. "Who did you say you were?"

". . . um . . . doctors?" I said in a voice intended to sound low and hefty, but that mostly squeaked.

Danny nodded vigorously. "Junior doctors."

"I see," the nurse said, eyeing us up and down. "I've had a report of a couple of students pretending to be doctors. Would you mind removing your masks?"

"Can't!" I blurted out.

"You *can't?* Why can't you?"

"Too many germs," Danny said. "Toxic. Very toxic. For instance, rubella."

"Ebola," I added.

"Ecoli."

"Epoxy."

"Enough!" Nurse Sternwood cried. "I'm losing my patience with you two."

I sucked air through my mask. "We're all going to lose patients if you don't let us deliver these pans!"

"Pans?" she said, as two orderlies came around the corner and into the hall. "Ah, yes. I heard one of these fake doctors is going around with a pile of pans."

"Well, you couldn't expect the pans to go around by themselves!" Danny said.

I think the next noise from the woman was a grunt.

"Where are you taking the pans?" she asked.

"Back to the kitchen," I said.

"These pans?" she said. "These . . . *bed*pans?"

I gulped. "*Bed*pans?"

Even behind his mask, I saw Danny's peachy cheeks go pale. "Well, that explains the smell. . . ."

His fingers went limp.

We were down the hall before the pans hit the floor.

Clang! Plonk! Splosh! They splattered everywhere.

"GET THEM!" Nurse Sternwood yelled to the orderlies.

"The bedpans?" the orderlies cried.

"THE KIDS!" she shouted. "GET THEM!"

[CUT BACK TO: school courtyard]

PAM

But mostly our first president is famous for laundry. He washed a ton of it. And that's why we call him . . . WASHINGTON!

There was a moment's stark silence in the courtyard. All you heard was the whirring of cameras.

It was a striking moment.

The next thing that struck was some kind of peach.

I don't know how long it had been since it was ripe, or what color it started out as, but it made some kind of ugly mess when it slapped Pam on the cheek.

SPLORT!

PAM

Agkk! Hey! It was all Maggio's fault!
He told me my essay was perfect!

"Perfect!?" Principal Pangborn's domey scalp turned purple. The twin furrinesses of his eyebrows became a single thick hedge over his nose. He began screaming.

PRINCIPAL PANGBORN

Why you . . . you . . . FAKE TEACHER!

For a second, all sound stopped.

Then the fake teacher leaped to the top of the podium, and ripped off his tweed jacket with the elbow patches.

Under it was a uniform of hospital blue.

MR. MAGGIO

I am . . . Nursing Home Security Cop!

And if I can't find Wiggins, I'll find a substitute!

His fiery eyes fixed on our own Principal Pangborn.

MR. MAGGIO

You! Baldy! You look like you could use a rest! In a rest home!

What happened next was like a Frankenstein mob scene. The air was thick with shrieks and flying peaches.
"I'LL GET YOU!" Maggio yelled at Pangborn.
"GET HIM!" Pangborn yelled at Maggio.
"GET HER!" the kids yelled at Pam.

[CUT BACK TO: Coconut Palms Rest Villa]

"GET THEM!" Nurse Sternwood yelled at us.
At that precise moment, Wiggy and Jay stormed up the hall. With them was Dr. Goodwin, leading an angry mob of patients toward Nurse Sternwood.

DR. GOODWIN

GET HER!

Mrs. Burke and her TV room friends spotted Danny.

139

MRS. BURKE
GET HIM—FOR US!

"Yikes!" Danny cried. "Spencer, this way!" He yanked the nearest door open, ran through it dragging me roughly after him, and slammed the door behind us.

The room was absolutely black inside.

"I can't see a thing!" I yelped, trying to feel along the wall for a light switch. "Danny, your flashlight! Give me some light—I don't want to fall on my face! Do the flick!"

Then I heard the horrible sound.

Flll . . . flll . . . flubb!

"Oww!"

"DO THE FLICK!" I screamed again.

"I can't! I blew my thumb out with the remote last night! I tried to do three shows at the same time! It was too much! I can't flick! I got no pressure!"

That's when my hands felt no pressure. On the wall.

Because—suddenly—there was no wall.

There was a window.

"Agkkk!"

I tumbled straight out onto the roof. I grabbed wildly for something to keep me from falling. All I found were loose tiles. Thanks to me pulling out those tiles before, a whole bunch of others had now come loose.

And I slid fast across them to the edge.

"DANNY! HELP ME!"

And then, there he was, the gripless flicking wonder boy, hurtling down at me, pushing me even faster over those rough tiles. Right to the edge of the roof.

It was too perfect. Then it got perfecter.

[SOUND EFFECTS: sound of ripping cloth: *KRRIPPPP!*]

"Agkkk!" I screamed again as we fell over the edge.

Just before my brain started flicking through the short comical show called *My Soon-To-Be-Ended Life*—

Thwump! Thwump!

We stopped falling and I found myself staring eye to eye with the bottom of a coffee cup!

"Ah!" said a voice. "Jay's java is the best!"

ME

Dickens?

Danny and I sat up on a wooden scaffold Dickens and Fenster had just put up to fix the roof tiles that I had loosened. Dickens smiled a weird smile.

"Hey kids. Where are your pants?"

I heard giggling from the parking lot. It was the camerawoman. "Perfect!" she said, her camera's red light flickering.

I sighed. "Can we fade out now? I'm hurt bad."

"I'm in a coma," Danny groaned.

The camerawoman punched her normal thumb up.

The red camera light went out.

And so did we.

FADE OUT:

END OF ACT TWO

CREDIT TAG

FADE IN:
SCENE 24: SCHOOL AUDITORIUM—FRIDAY A.M.

"So Mr. Maggio is still in the school somewhere?"

It was the next morning. Jay, Danny, Pam, and I were in the auditorium, where Mr. Shell was going to preview this week's show. The camerawoman was there already. Mr. Shell had told her to keep our faces in closeup through the whole scene.

"Maggio is still chasing the principal," Pam said. "Keeps yelling about new recruits for the Villa."

Danny laughed. "So he doesn't know Dr. Goodwin and the patients kicked Nurse Sternwood out?"

"Nope," said Jay. "And the best part is that

Wiggy and Mrs. Burke are helping to run Coconut Palms now."

"So cool," Pam said. "I heard they also made the SHARE program permanent with our school."

Jay nodded. "And on his day off, Wiggy's coming here to teach Mrs. Brady's classes."

"The part I still can't believe," Danny said, "is that the bad plumbing they found while digging in Jay's locker saved our school from a flood. How's that for luck?"

Jay pointed to himself. "I'm Pangborn's hero now for building my locker. He's gonna put my picture next to Washington's!"

Talk about weird conversations. I shook my head in absolute disbelief at what my friends were saying. "This is so amazing," I said. "I mean, sometimes things really *do* work out."

Danny turned to me. "Except for . . . you know."

"Right," I said. "Except for that." I glanced over at the camerawoman who was keeping us in closeup.

At that moment, the lights went down.

Leonard Shell strode out from behind the curtains, a cigar in each hand. "Nice show, kids. Lots of action. Loved it. In fact, I showed a preview to the *ER Cops* people. They're running scared.

They're thinking of moving their show to another night."

"Ha!" Danny yelped. "We flicked them!"

Mr. Shell chuckled. "Here's a preview of our episode. See what you think."

Light came from the back of the auditorium and the big pull-down screen onstage flickered.

"Ouch," I groaned.

And I continued groaning for the next twenty minutes. From the first scene to the last, the episode hurt.

It was mostly me, falling, jumping, and losing my pants. Oh, and the occasional losing of consciousness.

What struck me was that Mr. Shell rigged the laughtrack to blast out each time something embarassing happened to me.

Even my so-called friends doubled over at the final closeup of my face grinning a dopey grin as I sat on the workmen's scaffold.

With, of course, no pants on.

That got the biggest laugh.

"Danny was there, too," I said. "He was also pantless."

"But . . . I'm not the star," he said, faking humility.

The lights went up.

"You have to admit, though," Pam said. "Everything ended pretty well. Except for . . . you know."

I grunted and slapped the arm of my chair. "Yeah, I know. So, are all the loose ends tied up?"

"Not quite," Mr. Shell said. "In fact, we're taping the last scene upstairs right now. It's called the credit tag. That's where all the stories are tied up nice and neat. Go to the live cameras!"

A scene came into focus on the big screen.

SCENE: UPSTAIRS HALL

Mr. Maggio gallops after the principal, yelling.

MR. MAGGIO

I'll get you, Pangborn! You'll be a
patient if I have to put handcuffs
on you!

The two men are heading directly for the upstairs janitor's closet.

"That's the loft of Jay's locker condo!" Danny said.

I stared wide-eyed. "This is not going to be good."

At the last instant, Principal Pangborn twirls on his heels, opens the closet door, and steps aside.

PRINCIPAL PANGBORN

After you, Fakey!

Mr. Maggio slips on cheese drips and rotten peaches. He plummets into the dark depths before him.

[CUT TO: Mr. Maggio's terrified face, mouth open]

MR. MAGGIO

Ahhhhhh!

[SOUND EFFECTS: *THUMP! CRASH! BANG! CLONK!*]

PRINCIPAL PANGBORN

Talk about going down in history! Ouch!

MR. MAGGIO

You win, Pangborn! You win!

PRINCIPAL PANGBORN

Oh, I know.

[SOUND EFFECTS: resounding laughter!]

The principal quietly shuts the door, dusts his hands, and walks away with a big grin on his face.

FADE OUT.

We cheered for a long time.

"That was pretty amazing," I said. "The principal flicked Maggio right off his show."

"And into my locker," Jay said. "Too bad Dickens and Fenster took out the stairs. He might have had a softer landing."

Pam laughed. "I hated losing that contest, but it was worth it to see Principal Pangborn smile like that."

"Now school can get back to normal," Danny said.

I thought about that. "What would normal be like?"

Wham!

[CUT TO: back doors of auditorium, blasting open]

Perfectly on cue, the doors swung wide and a bunch of Mr. Maggio's former students charged down the center aisle toward us. They murmured and grunted like an angry mob. But judging from how slowly they charged, they seemed pretty tired of the whole thing.

Even the cameraman following them looked bored.

"There's Jay," Dee Weiden said flatly. "Get him."

Jay grinned suddenly. "Look at me, Danny. I'm on Dee's show now!"

"What!" Danny cried.

I blinked. "I thought the mob was after Pam?"

"They got me last night," Pam said. "I'd almost made it safely to Jay's locker, but I slipped on a peach that Dee threw. They'd be after me now, except for . . . you know."

"Right, I know," I said, slapping the arm of my chair again.

"So I'm pinch-hitting for her," Jay said, waving at the mob. "Okay, people, let's do it!"

Pam shrugged. "Yeah, Jay's my . . . substitute."

"Get him!" The Tank boomed. "Get the fake Pam!"

As the mob tramped after Jay, Dee passed by.

"Hi, Dee!" Danny said, looking up at her brightly.

She glanced down at him, opened her mouth, and . . . coughed. Then she walked on.

Danny's eyes lit up. "Did you see that? She no-ticed me! She may not like me, but she noticed me! I'm in her radar! She noticed! Ya—hoo!"

"She throws a good peach, too," Pam added, as we left the auditorium and entered the main hall, the camera still on our faces. "Speaking of peaches and loose ends, Danny, because you told Dee about my plan, I got you a gift. If it weren't for you, I wouldn't be in this—well, you know."

Danny's cheeks turned red. "Tell me you didn't—"

"Oh, but I did."

"Look, everybody, it's Danny The Flick!"

"Oh, man!" Danny groaned. We all turned to see Mrs. Burke motoring slowly up the hall in her wheelchair followed by a bunch of her TV-room chums.

"Flick, Danny, flick!" Pam said with a wild laugh.

[CUT TO: closeup of Danny's limp, bandaged thumb]

At the same instant, Principal Pangborn emerged from his office and spotted me. He raised his finger. "Ah, Spencer? About next week's show. I have an-other idea. . . ."

"We'd all better flick!" I cried.

Camera finally pulls back to reveal Pam and Danny and me <u>sitting in wheelchairs</u>. We flick our motors on and wheel slowly—so slowly—down the hall.

ME

VRRMM! VRRMM! VRRMMMMMM!

FADE OUT

END OF SHOW

The Spencer Babbitt Show is taped before a live audience at Preston Wodehouse Middle School in Hollywood, California

A Production of SHELLIVISION STUDIOS

About the Author

Believe it or not, TONY ABBOTT was born in Cleveland, Ohio, where his mom often found him watching television upside down. He's been doing things at odd angles ever since. Due to some weird genetic thing, Tony is able to recall every single event in his childhood. This has helped him to write more than two dozen funny novels for young readers, including the popular *Danger Guys* books.

Tony hopes to write an actual television show soon, but in the meantime he's penned *Don't Touch that Remote!* Each title in this series is designed as its very own *sitcom-in-a-book,* something Tony describes as his own "nifty" idea.

When not writing, reading, or visiting schools, Tony likes dreaming about shiny cars, piling cheesy toppings on his pizzas, and going down in elevators really really fast. He now lives in Connecticut with his lovely wife, two delightful daughters, and several thousand books, which he reads mostly right-side up.

It's TV—in a book!
Don't miss a single hilarious episode of—

Don't Touch that Remote!

Episode 1: Sitcom School
Spencer's got his own TV show!
Watch him try to keep his wacky co-stars out of trouble!

Episode 2: The Fake Teacher (November 1999)
Is that new teacher all he seems?
And is Jay hiding something really, really big?

Episode 3: Stinky Business (January 2000)
Danny's got a brand-new career, and something smells!
Here's a clue: It ain't fish!

Episode 4: Freak Week (March 2000)
It's the spookiest show ever as the gang spends overnight in
their school.
Will Pam's next laugh be her last?

Tune in as Spencer, Pam, Danny, and Jay negotiate the riotous
world of school TV. Laugh out loud at their screwball plots and
rapid-fire TV-style joking. Join in the one-liners as this over-the-
top, off-the-wall, hilarious romp leaves you screaming—
Don't Touch That Remote!

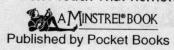

A MINSTREL® BOOK

Published by Pocket Books

2302

BRUCE COVILLE'S

The fascinating and hilarious adventures of the world's first purple sixth grader!

I WAS A SIXTH GRADE ALIEN

THE ATTACK OF THE TWO-INCH TEACHER

I LOST MY GRANDFATHER'S BRAIN
(Coming in November 1999)

PEANUT BUTTER LOVERBOY
(Coming in January 2000)

By Bruce Coville

Published by Pocket Books